ARMAGEDDON

Books by James Patterson
for Readers of All Ages

The Witch & Wizard Novels
Witch & Wizard (with Gabrielle Charbonnet)
The Gift (with Ned Rust)
The Fire (with Jill Dembowski)

The Maximum Ride Novels
The Angel Experiment
School's Out—Forever
Saving the World and Other Extreme Sports
The Final Warning
MAX
FANG
ANGEL
Nevermore

The Daniel X Novels
The Dangerous Days of Daniel X (with Michael Ledwidge)
Watch the Skies (with Ned Rust)
Demons and Druids (with Adam Sadler)
Game Over (with Ned Rust)
Armageddon (with Chris Grabenstein)

The Middle School Novels
Middle School, The Worst Years of My Life
(with Chris Tebbetts, illustrated by Laura Park)
Middle School: Get Me out of Here!
(with Chris Tebbetts, illustrated by Laura Park)

Other Illustrated Novels
Daniel X: Alien Hunter (graphic novel; with Leopoldo Gout)
Daniel X: The Manga, Vol. 1–3 (with SeungHui Kye)

For previews of upcoming books in these series and other information,
visit www.MaximumRide.com, www.Daniel-X.com,
www.WitchAndWizard.com, and www.MiddleSchoolBook.com.

For more information about the author, visit www.JamesPatterson.com.

DANIEL X

ARMAGEDDON

JAMES PATTERSON
AND CHRIS GRABENSTEIN

LITTLE, BROWN AND COMPANY
New York Boston

Copyright © 2012 by James Patterson

Little, Brown and Company

Hachette Book Group
237 Park Avenue, New York, NY 10017
Visit our website at www.lb-kids.com

Little, Brown and Company is a division of Hachette Book Group, Inc.
The Little, Brown name and logo are trademarks of Hachette Book Group, Inc.

The publisher is not responsible for websites (or their content) that are not owned by the publisher.

First Edition: October 2012

Library of Congress Cataloging-in-Publication Data

Patterson, James, 1947–
Armageddon / James Patterson and Chris Grabenstein. — 1st ed.
  p. cm. — (Daniel X ; 5)
  Summary: Daniel faces dastardly Number Two, who has slowly been amassing an underground army of aliens to help him enslave Earth's population in preparation for the arrival of Number One, the most powerful alien in the universe and Daniel's arch-nemesis.
  ISBN 978-0-316-10179-0
  [1. Extraterrestrial beings—Fiction. 2. Orphans—Fiction. 3. Science fiction.] I. Grabenstein, Chris. II. Title.
  PZ7.P27653Arm 2012
  [Fic] — dc23

2012005480

10 9 8 7 6 5 4 3 2 1

RRD-C

Printed in the United States of America

PROLOGUE

HIGH-OCTANE EVIL

One

I HAVE NEVER felt so alone in a crowd.

I was penned in, crushed by a horde of seriously evil thugs who, fortunately, didn't realize I had infiltrated their ranks. I surged with the teeming mob down a stifling corridor carved through a solid mass of black anthracite. Coal dust filled the air. And my lungs.

I did not belong here. Not in a million years.

Which might explain why I was so petrified.

Like the sea of murky shadows bobbing all around me, I was cloaked in a black robe with a pointed black hoodie — a cape I had quickly materialized so I could tag along with this legion of alien outlaw freaks.

Trust me: I *needed* to blend in.

If just one of these fiendish outlanders discovered I was Daniel X, it'd be time to open the orange marmalade.

I'd be toast.

Burnt, *black* toast.

After all, I am the Alien Hunter, legendary destroyer of

the universe's most evil extraterrestrials—including some of these goons' first and second cousins.

Disguised, and with my face hidden under my cloak, I moved with the murmuring rabble from the mineshaft into a foul and fiery chamber. The cavernous room looked like a dark cathedral. Jagged stalactites jutted out of the ceiling fifty feet up and oozed droplets of molten lava. Slick cave walls glistened with the light of a million flickering torch flames. A suffocating scent of sulfur tinged the acrid air.

Now I wasn't just petrified. I was also feeling kind of queasy. Sulfur, with its rotten-egg odor, has never been my favorite non-metal on the Periodic Table of Elements.

"Where are you from?" I heard a nearby alien grunt, luckily not to me.

"San Francisco. You?"

"Phnom Penh."

"Nairobi," snarled another.

These guys were definitely out-of-towners—from *way* out of town. Alien creatures from far-off galaxies. Extraterrestrial terrorists who lived, disguised as humans, all over the globe. And each and every one of these mutant monsters had come to this secret subterranean conclave to learn the same thing I had snuck down here to find out: Where on Earth were they preparing to strike next?

Suddenly a wall of fire shot up from an elevated stone platform at the center of the underground arena. A wave of cheers roared through the gathering as a gaseous fireball exploded and *Number 2 himself* stepped through the swirling whirlpool of smoke and flame.

That's right. Number 2. *Numero Dos.* The second-most-heinous villain on The List of Alien Outlaws currently residing on Earth.

I could tell instantly that this fiend had earned his second-seed ranking the hard way. All seven of my senses informed me that I was in the presence of pure, undiluted, high-octane evil. He looked the part, too. The demon astride the elevated stage towered over all the other beastly creatures. Enormous wings jutted out of his bony back. Red-hot rage seared his sunken eye sockets.

After momentarily savoring the adulation of his fawning fans, Number 2 raised both of his muscle-rippled arms to silence the crowd.

"My disciples! My cohorts! I have waited many centuries for this moment, this ultimate battle. Now, at last, my time has come! The final reckoning is at hand!"

The mob roared, stomped its feet, and shot up various tentacles and slimy appendages. Number 2 had his minions mesmerized.

All except this one stooge — Number 30-something on The List. I couldn't remember the gutbucket with the googly eyes' precise rank because, well, I tend to concentrate on the seriously twisted alpha dogs in the Top Ten, not the one-hit wonders down below.

Unfortunately, Mr. 30-whatever *was* concentrating his googly eyes on me.

In fact, he was staring straight at me, licking his slick amphibian lips and drooling.

"You!" he growled as he puffed out his enormous blow-frog chin and chest. I could tell: the toady bootlicker not only recognized me, he was all set to score some serious brownie points by ratting me out to his fearsome leader.

Too bad I never gave him that chance.

Señor 30-something had given me a pretty terrific idea by proudly puffing himself up like that. Since I was born with the awesome ability to rearrange matter at will—yeah, you copy that?—I quickly morphed the bulging blowhard into a hot-air balloon. Buffeted by thermals roiling up from the steamy horde below, the slick black blimp shot up toward the ceiling and all those pointy-tipped stalactites. He was definitely on his way to bursting his own bubble.

But he never made it that high.

The conventioneer from California whipped out his Bolide Blaster and, in a masterful display of indoor skeet shooting, torched the zeppelin in midair, initiating an awesome indoor fireworks display. The late Mr. 30-something exploded into a spectacular shower of fire flowers, glowing embers, and glittering streaks.

Raucous laughter, led by Number 2, echoed off the cavern walls.

My cover had not been blown, but the same could not be said for Mr. 30-something.

His cover—not to mention everything else—had been blown to bits.

Two

"PREPARE FOR ARMAGEDDON," hissed Number 2, his words dripping black-hearted viciousness. "It is time for the total annihilation!"

All around me, alien outlaw freaks were foaming at the mouth. Literally.

This was it, the moment they'd all been waiting for.

The one *I'd* been dreading.

"Attacks on Washington, New York, London, Paris, Moscow, and Beijing will soon commence. Los Angeles, Frankfurt, Rome, Chicago, and Tokyo will also tremble and fall. I will crush their small towns and villages: Ames, Iowa, and Marietta, Georgia. Edam in the Netherlands and Malacca in Malaysia. Not a single earthling will be spared as I lay waste to their so-called civilization."

As you can probably tell, Number 2 and his hench-lackeys had a pretty low opinion of humanity. Then again, I'm pretty sure none of them had ever bothered checking out Michelangelo's *David*, a Beethoven symphony, or an orange-and-white swirl cone down on the Jersey shore.

"This planet is ripe for the taking," the demon continued, his voice cold, confident, and eerily intelligent. "The human race has never been more divided, more shortsighted, more consumed with greed, or more inflamed by religious differences. Before I am through, all of humanity will hail me as their new Lord and Master. They will gladly embrace all that I believe in and become my slaves."

The crowd growled its approval.

Number 2 silenced them with a simple, savage flick of the wrist. "There is, however, one who has the power to stop all I seek to accomplish. A young boy. A teenager."

A few of his henchbeasts dared to laugh, until Number 2 glared at them with his red-hot laser-pointer eyes. Suddenly sizzling red beams shot out of the leader's eyes and threw the laughing monsters halfway across the cavern, where they remained motionless on the ground.

"If you fear me—and you should—then fear this child! He has already destroyed many of the universe's most powerful warriors. Never underestimate his abilities because of his youth." He gestured at the gargantuan cloud of gray smoke billowing up behind him. "Never underestimate Daniel X!"

Right on cue, my mug shot flashed into view on that thirty-foot-tall smoke screen. I was squinting, had a zit near my nose, and basically looked like a total scrungrow. They must've found the yearbook from the one school where I actually hung around long enough for picture day.

"Find him," said Number 2, his voice weirdly serene. "Bring Daniel to me and, rest assured, I *will* destroy him."

Needless to say, destroying Number 2 was high on *my* to-do list, too. But I had to wonder: Was there really any conceivable way for me, a teenager, to stop him, a lethally powerful alien commanding an army of murderous minions?

And what did this say about Number 1? If Number 2 could command a force this enormous, how huge was Number 1's army?

"You will receive further instructions in due course," said Number 2 as his wings creaked open. "For the present, your mission is quite simple: Find the boy. Bring him to me."

All around me, grotesque alien beings sprouted webbed wings and collapsed into themselves as if they were gray, gauzy umbrellas. I quickly realized what was going on: Number 2's storm troopers were turning themselves into *Diphylla ecaudata.*

Vampire bats.

In an instant, I was surrounded by thousands upon thousands of unbelievably ugly, bloodsucking, wing-flapping, furry fiends—all of them shrieking with glee.

Well, you know what they say: When in hell, do as the hellions do.

Totally focused on all things flying mammalian, I used my transformative powers to turn myself into a bloodthirsty bat. My nose shriveled down into a pug muzzle. My teeth sharpened into fangs. My ribs crunched out to form the articulated skeletal scaffolding for a pair of thin-skinned wings.

When all I could see was a glowing green radar screen, I squealed, fluttered out my webbed wings, and flew back up that mineshaft with the rest of the repulsively scuzzy flock.

Honestly? The whole bat thing was pretty disgusting.

I don't know how Bruce Wayne deals with it.

PART ONE
THE GATHERING SWARM

Chapter 1

TIME FOR ALIEN Hunter Tip Number 46: Always have an exit strategy, preferably one that doesn't involve transforming yourself into a flying rodent with rusty-gutter breath from guzzling way too much iron-rich hemoglobin.

Coming out of the bat transformation, I felt wiped. My mind was totally blown. My retinas had burnt-in blip spots from doing time as radar screens.

But at least I was me again.

I had lost the black cloak and the bat wings. I was back in a T-shirt, blue jeans, and sneakers, catching my breath outside a cave entrance. I had come to this abandoned West Virginia coal mine after picking up a hot tip on Number 2's possible location. The intel had been solid. I had definitely found the despicable Deuce's hidey-hole. My next problem: What to do about him, not to mention his massive army? How could I stop these extraterrestrial terrorists from destroying every city, town, and village on their hit list?

Still groggy, I retrieved my backpack, which I'd hidden deep inside a rock niche outside the cave. I fished out the super-thin, higher-than-high-tech alien laptop that has been my mission bible since day one and flipped open the lid. I needed to consult The List of Alien Outlaws on Terra Firma, which is what those of us from other parts of the galaxy call Earth.

I also needed to recharge my batteries. For me to rearrange molecules to create whatever my imagination cooks up, I need to be super calm and concentrate like crazy. If I'm tired or cranky, forget about it. At that moment I don't think I could've materialized a Double Whopper with cheese, even though I sort of wished I could. Bats burn up a ton of calories, what with the wing flapping and all that internalized radar action. I was famished.

The List thrummed to life in my lap. Much to my surprise, Balloon Boy—the bloated bullfrog I had called 30-something—was actually Number 29. Guess the freak-azoid had shot up a slot or two after I erased a couple of his superiors in alien hunts past.

However, slot 29 was as high as Floating Froggy would ever hop. The constantly self-updating List was already flashing TERMINATED next to his name and number.

I swiped my fingers through the air and The List, fully annotated with illustrations, scrolled up the screen to exactly what I needed to see.

The entry for Number 2.

For some bizarre-o reason, the computer continued to pretty much draw a blank on the guy. Yes, there was a list of his known physical appearances (apparently he was a world-class shape-shifter, just like me), but under Planet of Origin, all I saw was CLASSIFIED. Same thing with Evil Deeds Done. CLASSIFIED. Powers? CLASSIFIED.

Classified? Hello, computer—you work for *me*, remember?

I gave the computer a good whack on the side. Yes, it's an extremely low-tech solution, but one that sometimes works, even with the galaxy's coolest, most artificially intelligent gizmos.

Not this time. The images on the screen refused to budge. Number 2's background would remain a mystery. A CLASSIFIED mystery.

I realized I needed to forget about where Number 2 came from and what he had already done, and focus instead on where he said he was going (all over the planet) and what he planned on doing once he and his army got there (wiping out human civilization and enslaving millions, not to mention making my life totally miserable).

Still glued to the uncooperative computer screen, I felt a not-so-gentle tap on my shoulder.

Startled, I whipped around.

Suddenly I was face-to-face-to-face-to-face with a four-sided killing machine.

Chapter 2

"WELL, WELL, WELL, well," the thing said, chortling in quadraphonic surround sound.

Then all of the blockhead's faces grinned.

"How frightfully convenient! Number 2 commissions us to go find Daniel X and, lo and behold, I find you hiding right outside our super-secret meeting place."

I, of course, immediately recognized the cubic jerkonium. It was hard not to. The creature was a four-sided warrior from the planet Varladra, complete with two pairs of brutal arms clutching four extremely lethal weapons: a scimitar the size of a scythe, a quarto-headed battle-ax, a classic nine-ring Chinese broadsword, and—just in case he got tired of flailing his limbs and swinging steel—what looked like a semi-automatic, rapid-repeating disintegrator gun.

Having just eyeballed The List, I knew exactly who (make that *what*) I was dealing with: Number 33 in my top forty countdown.

"Prepare to die, traitor!" sneered the clanking cube.

"No thanks," I said. "By the way, is Rubik your uncle or your aunt?"

He growled and swung his ax, aiming for my head like my neck was the tee and my skull the ball.

I ducked into a crouch. He whiffed.

"*Stee-rike* one," I said.

Number 33 rotated ninety degrees to the left, jangling the belt of human and alien skulls he wore wrapped around his squarish waist. Swishing blades twirled and whirled on all sides of his chest. It was like fighting a berserk food processor. The boxy behemoth only had two stubby legs, but both were mounted on rolling swivels. Number 33 was definitely turning out to be hell on wheels.

He tried a downward log-splitting lumberjack chop with the battle-ax—the one with *four* razor-sharp blades.

I was supposed to be the log.

I rolled right. Again, he whiffed.

"*Stee-rike* two!"

He yanked his ax head out of the dirt with one arm and used two of the others to swing his Chinese broadsword and slash at me with the scimitar.

I dodged, then ducked.

Two swings. Two misses.

"*Stee*-rikes three and four!"

I guess the official rules of baseball are different on Varladra, because he kept taking swings. I kept countering: juking and sidestepping, bobbing and weaving.

I needed to figure out this creep's weakness, and fast.

Fighting this four-sided death machine was a lot like taking on four Attila the Huns at the same time.

I darted left to avoid a flying triple parry and follow-up double thrust.

Man, the guy's aim was definitely off. Maybe he needed four pairs of glasses for his four pairs of eyes. Maybe he was still blind as a bat.

I checked out his flat noses, swarthy complexion, and wispy Fu Manchu beards.

Wait a second.

Number 33 *was* Attila the Hun, one of the most fearsome Eurasian nomads to ever invade Rome and earn the name "Barbarian." Or he *had* been Attila, back in the early to mid fifth century. All he needed was a fur-lined helmet and a woolly vest. This killing machine had been on Earth for sixteen centuries and he'd never been beaten. Talk about your heavyweight champion of the world.

"Stand still, boy!" Attila growled at me. "Do not prolong the inevitable."

"What's the matter, *hon?*" I said, still flitting around like a hummingbird stoked on liquid sugar. I couldn't resist the pun. "Have a rough day pillaging and plundering?"

Cube-head sneered at me. I could see chunks of meat snagged between his rotting teeth.

"Prepare to die, weakling!"

"Sorry. No way am I letting you and your mongrel horde of mutant misfits destroy human civilization."

"Foolish boy! This planet belongs to whoever or whatever is strong enough to take it!"

"Or defend it!"

Attila swiped a couple of hands roughly across a few of his slobbering mouths.

"Enough," he said. "It is suppertime, and I am most hungry. Therefore, submit to me and die!"

Up came the disintegrator gun.

Good thing I finally figured out how to beat this guy.

In a flash, I turned myself into a bubbling hot pot of yak stew.

Yum.

Chapter 3

ATTILA THE GORILLA must've been seriously starving.

He immediately grabbed the pot of meaty yak gruel and tossed it into his mouth. That is, he grabbed *me* and threw me down his gullet in a single gulp.

Over the teeth, over the gums, look out stomach, here I come.

I slid into his esophagus and cannonballed down the quivering chute into his gut.

They say the way to an alien's heart is through his stomach, and that was my plan: get digested, clog his arteries, and attack his heart!

Of course, when they say that thing about the stomach and heart, they leave out the bit about how, in between, you have to spend a little quality time down in the bowels. Remember to hold your nose when we get there.

I splashed into a pool of burbling acid and bobbed around with milky chunks of half-digested french fries, the gooey remains of a Snickers bar, and what might've once been creamed corn. Attila's stomach looked exactly like that Rubbermaid barrel full of pig slop the high school cafeteria guy scrapes all the dirty dishes into.

I sloshed forward, trying to avoid a McNugget oil slick. I needed to act like a bran muffin and move things along his digestive tract—fast. So I swam downstream as quickly as yak stew can.

Now, in order for me to get into Number 33's bloodstream and give him some serious heartburn, I needed to be a nutrient by the time I reached his small intestine. If not, my whole plan (and me with it) would go straight down the toilet. Literally.

As I was funneled into the stomach's exit ramp, I transformed myself into a glob of yak fat and, after a quick bile bath, moved into the small intestine. I thought I might hurl. The narrow, undulating tube smelled worse than any sewer I've ever had the pleasure of crawling through.

Fortunately, I didn't have to deal with the bowel stench for long, because I was instantly sucked through the intestinal lining. Just like that, I was cruising through Number 33's circulatory system.

If I could make it into his arteries—which had to be unbelievably clogged with sixteen hundred years' worth of Mongolian barbecue, mutton dumplings, and fried goat cheese—maybe I could completely block a blood vessel and shut his heart down.

Upstream, I could hear his heart muscle pounding out a four-four beat like a quartet of thundering kettledrums.

Because he had four hearts!

If I blocked the blood flow to one, the other three might be able to compensate.

Okay. I needed a plan B, as in "Blow up" or "ka-Boom."

The vein I was log-flume riding through splashed me down inside one of Attila's throbbing hearts. As I shot through one of its valves, I made myself morph again.

I hung on to the flapping valve with both hands as I began to change back into me—the full-sized, five-foot-ten Daniel X. I started to expand inside his cramped heart chamber like one of those Grow Your Own Girlfriend sponge toys that's guaranteed to grow 600 percent when you soak it in a bowl of water overnight.

Only I grew much bigger and much faster. Call it a teenage growth spurt.

I shattered his heart and burst through that alien's ribcage like the alien in *Alien*.

Blood spurting all around me (picture ketchup squeeze bottles gone wild), I watched Number 33—gasping and gurgling and clutching what was left of his chest—topple to the ground.

Attila the Hun was now Attila the Done.

Meanwhile, I was a little wet, somewhat sticky, and totally grossed out.

But I would live to fight another day. And another alien.

Number 2.

Clearly the most formidable and fearsome foe I have ever faced.

Chapter 4

SO WHAT WOULD you say is humankind's greatest creation?

Language? Music? Maybe art?

All excellent choices. But if you ask me, the greatest thing any creature anywhere ever created is a concept called "friendship."

I guess my four friends are my greatest creation, too. Without your friends, well, what are you?

"You guys," said Joe, "this funnel cake is awesome."

"It's cold," said Dana.

"And your point is?" Joe took another chomp out of the web of chewy fried dough dusted with powdered sugar and drenched with squiggles of chocolate sauce.

"You're basically eating knotted flour and lard, Joe," Emma said. "It's not very good for your heart."

Having just examined the insides of the late Number 33's cardiovascular plumbing up close and personal, I realized Emma, my earth-mother health-nut friend, had a point.

"Well, it may not be good for my heart, but it is *excellent* for my mouth," said Joe, who had an iron stomach to rival Attila's. My friend has been known to order "one of everything" at Pizza Hut. But no matter how much chow he wolfs down on a regular basis, he stays super skinny. Talk about an excellent metabolism.

This was what I needed; nothing renews my creative juices like hanging out and goofing around with my buds. And we weren't just in the middle of a pig-out session at the local county fair. No, my four best friends and I were in the middle of Six Flags Over Georgia.

After my Thrilla with Attila, I decided to call up Joe, Emma, Willy, and Dana and head south to do a little recon on Marietta, Georgia—one of the smaller towns on Number 2's Places to Destroy/Humans to Enslave list. Aliens are much easier to smell outside your major metropolitan areas—fewer competing odors.

Okay, I could've gone to Ames, Iowa. But the nearest amusement park to Ames is Adventureland, home to lots of incredible waterslides, and after slipping and sliding through Number 33's wet and wild circulatory system I was more in the mood for roller coasters. Six Flags Over Georgia has *eleven* of 'em.

Oh, something else you should probably know, in case you haven't already figured it out: When I say I "called up" my friends, I don't mean I hit speed dial on my iPhone. I mean my four best friends since forever are 100-percent pure *products of my imagination*. It's not like I walk around talking to invisible, make-believe buddies. When Joe, Emma,

Willy, and Dana are around, everybody can see them, hear them, and, in Joe's case, smell them. But not one of my friends would exist if I didn't imagine him or her first.

I realize my special talent may seem alien to you but, then again, you weren't born on my home planet, Alpar Nok. For me, the power to create (the most awesome superpower of them all, btw) is just part of my genetic code.

Without this amazing gift, I'd be totally alone in your world.

And alone is never a good place to be when dealing with the likes of Number 2.

"Hey, you guys," said Willy, coming around the base of the Dare Devil Dive coaster to join us. "I scouted it out. We're the only ones here! The place is totally ours!"

"Well, duh," said Dana. "It's after three AM. The park's closed."

"Hmm," said Joe, licking sugar and chocolate sauce off his fingers, "must be why the funnel cakes are stone cold. Hey, you guys ever eat cold pizza for breakfast?"

"Yeah, right," said Dana with an eye roll. "Whenever possible, Joe."

"You should try it, Dana," said Willy. "When pizza's cold, the cheese stays locked in place."

"No sauce drippage, either," added Joe.

"By the way," said Willy, jabbing a thumb over his shoulder, "the new coaster looks absolutely amazing."

"I believe the Dare Devil Dive coaster is the Southeast's tallest beyond-vertical roller coaster," said Emma, who had picked up a bunch of brochures and maps when we first entered the amusement park.

"Hey, Daniel," teased Dana, who, full disclosure, I have a mad crush on. "Part of the park is called 'Gotham City.' You wanna head over there and check out this cool coaster called Batman: The Ride?"

"More bats?" I said. "No thanks."

"Let's do the Dare Devil Dive!" said Willy. "Get this: you climb ten stories up a vertical lift, then plummet down a ninety-five-degree first drop!"

"Um," said Dana, "not to barf all over your idea, Willy, but I detect one slight problem."

"What?"

Dana gestured at the dark rides towering all around us. "Like I said, it's after three AM."

"So?" said Willy, who can be as stubborn as he is brave.

"The park is closed, Willy," said Emma, who was Willy's little sister and knew him better than anybody. "You can't ride the rides, because, well, Six Flags very wisely shuts off all its electricity after hours in an attempt to conserve energy."

I smiled. "Well, you know what they say: it's a whole 'nother park after dark. Start 'em up!"

And, by the power of sheer imagination, I made every single ride in Six Flags whir back to life!

Chapter 5

YOU KNOW HOW when you go to an amusement park in the middle of the summer and you want to ride the really cool rides, but you have to wait like two hours in a line that keeps switching back on itself, so all you can do is keep staring at the hundreds of people ahead of you?

Well, this was absolutely *nothing* like that.

When we came to the end of any ride, we didn't have to unload and run around to the entrance to ride it again. I just imagined the thing starting up and—*ZAP!*—it did.

We defied gravity, flew through loop-the-loops, felt g-forces similar to those encountered during the reentry phase of interplanetary space travel, and, basically, got to retaste what we had for lunch that day when it flew back up into our mouths.

"C'mon, you guys," said Willy. "Time to take the ultimate plunge: the Dare Devil Dive coaster."

Yes, nausea fans, we'd been saving Six Flags' most incredible thrill ride for last.

We hurried over to the base of the bright yellow-and-red roller coaster. The logo emblazoned on its glowing two-story marquee sort of reminded me of Number 2 and his minions: a helmeted, goggled head with wings sprouting out on both sides and flames blazing up in the background.

"You okay, Daniel?" Emma asked when she caught me staring up at the wicked imagery.

"Yeah. Come on. Let's give this devil his due."

Our six-seater roller-coaster car was shaped like a fighter jet.

"Buckle up," said Emma. "Keep your feet and hands inside the car at all times."

"Your funnel cakes, too," Dana added, elbowing Joe.

"Blast us off, Daniel!" said Willy.

Of course roller coasters don't actually *blast* off. They kind of creep to a start and haul you up a hill. Coaster cars don't have engines, so the ride is totally powered by the energy stored up when the car climbs the track's first hill. After that, gravity and some other principles of physics are all you need.

A hidden chain hauled us straight up toward the starlit sky. When we were perched at the peak of the ten-story tower with our fighter plane's nose hanging over the edge, the ride seemed to stall.

"Is it busted?" asked Willy.

"Nope," said Joe, our technical wizard. "Teetering on the edge like this is just part of the coaster engineer's grand desiii…"

28

Joe didn't get to finish that thought.

We plummeted downward into a ninety-five-degree drop, which, check your protractors, is beyond straight down. We were actually angling *inward* as we dove straight for the ground.

With all sorts of kinetic energy rocketing us along, we careened up through three inversions, caught air on a zero-gravity hill, and swooped through an Immelmann U-turn—a half loop, half twist with a curving exit in the opposite direction from which we entered. (Quick fact: the whole move is based on a maneuver first employed by a German fighter pilot named Immelmann in World War I.) We raced into another nose-down dive, then shot up into a heartline roll (a total 360 where the pivot point is your heart, not your feet) before the car was slowed by magnetic brakes.

"Whahoobi!" shouted Willy.

"Un-*be*-lievable," added Joe, with a burp.

"I'm glad it's over," said Emma.

"Me, too," said Dana.

"I need liquid refreshment," said Joe.

Which gave me a wild idea. "Coming right up!"

Hey, if this ride was powered by my imagination, there were no limits, no magnetic brakes to slow me down. Defying gravity and tapping into my personal reserves of energy, I made the fighter jet car fly off the rails and soar across the amusement park.

"Daniel?" said Emma. "This wasn't in the brochure."

"It should be!" Willy shouted as we zipped underneath

the Sky Bucket gondola ride and landed on the tracks of the giant steel coaster called Goliath, a ride so humongous it wouldn't completely fit on the park grounds, so Six Flags had to run the track outside and back again. We rode up its two-hundred-foot ascent, zoomed through a couple of zero-gravity drops, slid into a giant spiral, and, since this was Daniel X's version of Goliath, flew off the tracks again so we could soar up into the sky.

"Hey, I can see Atlanta!" Joe said as I made the car climb higher than Goliath's highest hill. *Much* higher.

"I can see Miami," said Dana.

We did a couple of barrel rolls over the Mind Bender, buzzed the Dodge City Bumper Cars, and, for my big finish, made a smooth water landing in a turquoise blue river at Splash Water Falls just as the rapids sluiced around a bend to slide us down a five-story waterfall.

"You want liquid refreshment?" I joked to Joe. "Here it comes!"

"Woo-hoo!" shouted Willy. "Hang on!"

Our roller-coaster car plunged over the falls, hit the waiting water below, and sent up a ten-foot wall of foam and spray that drenched us all.

Totally soaked and laughing hysterically, we drifted along until our fighter plane bumped into some rubber dock guards and sloshed to a full stop.

"Let's do it again," said Willy. "Let's do it again." He sounded exactly like everybody's annoying little brother and/or sister.

Only we couldn't ride any more rides.

We weren't the only ones in the park anymore.

A squad of goons in bright white space suits leaped out of the surrounding pines and came charging up the exit ramp at us.

They were all carrying weapons.

Alien weapons.

Chapter 6

I COUNTED AT least a dozen storm troopers decked out in full-encapsulation bunny suits.

Their bodies were wrapped in loose-fitting, crinkly white fabric; their hands and feet were sealed inside black rubber gloves and boots; and their faces were hidden behind hoods and respirator masks.

They were carrying some pretty heavy artillery, too, none of it forged on planet Earth. We're talking RJ-57 over-the-shoulder, tritium-charge bazookas; high-intensity microwave guns; shock-wave cannons; blasters; and a pair of Opus 24/24s, which contain an illegal molecular resonator that fires a pulse vibrating at the precise frequency of its victim's neurotransmissions, causing the target to expire from sheer, unadulterated pain.

It's no wonder the Opus 24/24 is banned across most of the civilized universe.

"We can take these marshmallow people," Willy said, crouching into an arms-raised attack stance.

"No weapons, Daniel," urged Emma.

"We've got your back, bro," said Joe, moving to my right.

I eased into a neutral Aikido position, a nonaggressive martial arts style my father once taught me, and sized up the intruders. Aikido is all about redirecting the attackers' force into throws, locks, and restraints. I wasn't really sure how good it would be going up against an Opus 24/24, but I'd give it a whirl.

"Down on your knees, all of you," said the alien team leader, his reedy voice blaring out of a speaker embedded in his helmet. "Hands behind your heads. Do it! Now!"

"You guys?" I said to my friends. "You need to go."

"Let's lay down some hurt on these dudes," said Willy, wound up and ready to swing into full *Kung Fu Panda* mode. "And fast. I want to ride that X coaster again!"

"Not gonna happen," I said. "Not today."

"Wait one minute," protested Dana. "These...*things* have weapons."

Which was exactly why I needed to send my four friends away. Yes, I created them from memories stored in my mind, but they were extremely real. Therefore, an Opus 24/24 blast to any one of them would be extremely painful. I couldn't stand to see my friends get hurt like that.

"Later, you guys," I said.

"No," Dana said, actually stomping her feet. "You're in trouble. You need us. You can't just snap your fingers and send us away."

Well, yes, I could.

And I didn't need to snap my fingers, although I guess I could've. It might've looked more magical, might've fooled the heavy-breathing, space-suited cretins into thinking they were dealing with a witch or a wizard.

Instead, I just imagined my friends gone. To someplace safe. Someplace fun. I picked Six Flags Magic Mountain, outside of Los Angeles.

Maybe Willy *would* get to ride that ride again.

Chapter 7

THE SHRINK-WRAPPED SQUADRON leaped back a half step when Joe, Willy, Dana, and Emma vanished.

"Take a hint, guys," I said to the small army circled around me. "Do like my friends just did. Disappear."

"I said *on your knees*, son," grunted the lead goon through his helmet radio.

Interesting. He called me "son," but I knew he wasn't my dad, because when my father pops in for a surprise training seminar, he seldom travels with a posse of weapon-toting thugs.

And just to get you up to speed: my father, my mother, and my little sister, Pork Chop, have something in common with my four best friends—they exist only as living, breathing creations of my very vivid imagination.

"Son, let's not make this any more difficult than it has to be," said the robot-voiced squad commander.

Okay, he did that "son" thing again. I knew that none

of Number 2's battling barbarians would bother politely addressing me like family.

Who are these guys? I wondered.

Fortunately, a storm trooper to my left made a seriously stupid move with his weapon that sent my personal danger alert plummeting to DEFCON Zero.

The doofus was carrying his double-barreled benzene-powered vaporizer *backward*! If he squeezed the trigger, he'd fry himself to a crispy, crackly crunch. These guys weren't aliens. They were amateurs.

"Who are you people?" I asked.

"FBI. On your knees. Now."

"Sorry," I said. "I'm not big on bowing down before people, especially when they're dressed up like oversized FedEx envelopes."

"I repeat: We are with the FBI."

"Really? I guess that makes sense, if FBI stands for Freak Boy Institute."

"You want me to cuff the smart mouth?" barked another one of the guys in what I now recognized to be hazmat suits, those Tyvek outfits people wear to clean up nuclear meltdowns, biological waste, chemical spills — that sort of thing. Tough Guy slung his weapon over his shoulder and brandished a pair of FlexiCuffs so he could hog-tie my hands behind my back.

I focused on the plastic straps.

And turned them into strawberry Twizzlers.

Chapter 8

"WHAT THE..."

Tough Guy dropped the Twizzlers like they were glowing strands of red-hot plutonium.

"Okay, son," said the leader, making a big show of lowering his weapon. "We're impressed. We know what you're capable of. We're special agents with the FBI's IOU."

"IOU?" I laughed. "You're making that up, right? Like *I owe you*?"

"I assure you, son, this is not a joke. The Interplanetary Outlaw Unit functions under the radar as a liaison between the United States federal government and visitors from planets unknown."

"Like me, you mean?"

"No, son. We're on the same team."

Impossible, I thought. In all my battles with alien outlaws, never once had the United States cavalry come riding over the ridge to my rescue.

"We're your friends," he continued.

"No. My friends just left so you wouldn't hurt them with that Opus 24/24—if you even know how to fire it."

"We're not here to hurt anyone."

"Then tell me: Why are you carrying a weapon known to be the galaxy's most heinous, most hurtful, not to mention most outlawed, instrument of pain?"

"We thought carrying the alien weaponry would prove that we are who and what we claim to be. We confiscated these weapons in firefights."

"Right. The IOU. A super-secret branch of the FBI that deals with alien outlaws, just like Mulder and Scully used to on *The X-Files*. 'The truth is out there' and all that. Sorry, Agent, I want to *believe*, but, frankly, I don't."

"You should, Daniel. I promise you, I'm telling you the truth."

"Okay. That was good, calling me Daniel. I only have one question: How did you know my name?"

"Easy," said a tall man who stepped out of the shadows. "I told them."

Chapter 9

THIS NEW ARRIVAL wasn't wearing a hazmat suit or a sealed helmet.

In fact, he was wearing a two-piece suit so rumpled it looked like he had slept in it for maybe a month.

"Come on, guys," the tall man said to the others. "Put away those weapons before you hurt somebody. You act like you've never met an alien before."

All around me, weapons clattered as they were lowered. Clearly, the guy without a helmet, mask, or respirator was the man in charge.

"Daniel, I'm Special Agent Martin Judge. I head up the FBI's IOU, which, yes, is a lame name, but we're stuck with it. It's already printed on all our top secret business cards."

"Okay, Agent Judge," I said. "Same question for you: How, exactly, do *you* know my name?"

"Also easy, Daniel: I knew your mother and father."

"Impossible."

"Graff, Atrelda, and I worked together."

I had to hand it to the guy; he was pretty good. Graff (my father) and Atrelda (my mom) aren't your standard-issue parental-unit names—even in California, where people call one another stuff like Sunshine and Moonbeam. Special Agent Martin Judge had definitely done his homework.

I wondered for an instant if my mom and dad had ever filed an income-tax return, which would have put their names into the massive federal database. Maybe they filled out a census form. If so, I'd *love* to see what they put down for "race" and "ethnicity," since *Alpar Nokian* is never one of the standard check boxes.

"I was at your house several times for supper," Judge continued. "I never once had to wear a hazmat suit." This he said while shaking his head at his agents, who still refused to peel off their protective gear.

"Really? What'd my mom cook for you?"

"Pancakes, of course."

"For dinner?"

Judge shrugged. "You ever taste your mom's griddle cakes, Daniel?"

I played it nonchalant. "Once or twice." Truth is, my mother makes the most amazing flapjacks in this or any other galaxy.

"Pancakes that exceptional cannot and should not be confined to breakfast," said Judge.

"And where exactly did these pancake suppers take place, Agent Judge?"

"Like I said, Stinky Boy—at your house."

Okay, this was getting seriously weird. How did a special agent from the Federal Bureau of Investigation know my childhood nickname? The one my relatives had given me back on Alpar Nok, when I was what Huggies might call a toddler and my diapers were anything but snug or dry?

"I'm impressed with your research, Agent Judge."

"It's not research, Daniel. It's memory." He tapped his nose. "I helped your dad change you once when you were maybe two years old. You guys were living in Kansas at the time, remember?"

I froze.

Of course I remembered Kansas.

Kansas is where my mother and father were murdered.

Chapter 10

I WISH THAT I didn't sometimes, but of course I remember everything about that cursed, unspeakably horrible night back in Kansas.

I was three years old, playing in the basement of our home, building the Seven Wonders of the World out of Play-Doh. Yeah, this power-to-create-whatever-I-imagine thing kicked in way early, during my childhood development process.

Upstairs, I heard a horribly deep and strangled voice.

"The List! The List! Where is it?"

That heinous creature known as The Prayer (still Number 1 on The List of Alien Outlaws on Terra Firma) was upstairs attacking my parents. Later, the foul beast would come after me, and I will never forget what it looked like: a six-and-a-half-foot-tall praying mantis with a stalklike neck and stringy red dreadlocks hanging down between its antennae.

Upstairs, I heard my mother sobbing, and my father

pleading calmly: "Wait, hold on....Lower the gun, my friend. I'll get The List for you. I have it nearby."

"The List is *here*?" the deep voice boomed once again.

"Yes," said my father. "Now, if you'll just lower the—"

The next thing I heard was a string of deafening explosions. *Shooting.* I realized, in a flash of instantaneous knowledge, that the weapon being deployed was an Opus 24/24.

Guess you understand now why I totally hate the fiendish things.

I know the pain they can inflict, what they can destroy. *My whole world.*

Chapter 11

I PRETENDED THAT I had a mild case of the sniffles brought on by an allergy to Georgia pine pollen and quickly swiped the back of my hand across my face. I didn't want Special Agent Judge, or any of the other Fibbies, to see the tears welling up in my eyes.

"What do you want from me?" I asked.

"We need your help, Daniel. Like my guys told you, the IOU is a top secret covert unit operating within the Federal Bureau of Investigation. Our mission is to seek out and establish working relations with any and all friendly extraterrestrials residing in the United States of America."

"And the unfriendlies?" I asked, knowing there were a jillion more of those here on Earth than peace-loving planet-hoppers like me.

"The unfriendlies," said Judge, "we seek out and, whenever possible, terminate."

I gestured toward the agent who had been holding his

double-barreled vaporizer backward. "Really? How's that been working out for you?"

My question made Agent Judge wince.

"Not very well, Daniel. Not without the expert assistance of Protectors such as your father, your mother, and, now, you."

"Look," I said. "Why should I help you guys?"

"Because Number 2 is planning something big. What it is exactly…well, frankly, we don't know."

Because the IOU hadn't been able to infiltrate the demon's underground pep rally, like I had. I knew exactly what Number 2 had up his sleeve: the destruction of cities and towns all across the globe, coupled with the enslavement of the entire human population—all seven billion of 'em.

Judge tugged a simple silver chain out from under his shirt.

"I wanted to show you this, Daniel."

"What is it?" I asked. "A Saint Jude medal? Because Jude is the patron saint of hopeless causes, and if you ask me…"

I shut up when I saw what Agent Judge held in his hand.

"Where'd you get that?" I asked.

"Your father gave it to me."

It was a silver elephant pendant, an emblem of Alpar Nokian homeworld solidarity. My mother and father both received them when they graduated from the Academy and accepted positions in the Interplanetary Protectorship.

One of my earliest memories: I'm in my crib. My mother is singing me a lullaby. The silver elephant pendant dangles from her necklace.

Little-known factoid: Elephants were brought to Earth about three million years ago. From my planet. They were Alpar Nok's gift to Terra Firma. So, if you're taking notes, jot this down: Elephants are aliens, too. *Friendly* aliens.

Agent Judge gripped the silver pachyderm tightly in his fist.

"Earth has never needed assistance from the Interplanetary Protectorship more. And you're the best Alien Hunter to ever come out of Alpar Nok."

I blushed when Agent Judge said that. Turning bright red at the drop of a compliment? It's one of my most well-developed alien skills.

"Really?" I said. "Where'd you hear that?"

"Your father. He took me aside one day and said, 'Martin, keep an eye on Daniel. One day, my son will make all of Alpar Nok proud. He will grow up to become an Alien Hunter's Alien Hunter.'"

Now my ears had gone to code purple, and of course my heart was lodged in my throat because I was thinking about how my father never *really* got to see what kind of kid I turned out to be.

How he would never know what sort of man I might become.

"But I'm only a teenager, sir," I mumbled.

Agent Judge winked at me. "Well, for the sake of the planet and all humanity, let's hope you grow up real fast.

Come on, Daniel. We need to leave here ASAP. I'm afraid the time for fun and games is over. We need to deal with Number 2."

Agent Judge turned and headed down the Splash Water Falls exit ramp. His crew of hazmat guys followed after him. I hesitated.

"So, where exactly are we all going?" I called out.

"Kentucky. You need to meet Xanthos."

"O-kay. And who, if you don't mind me asking, is Xanthos?"

"Your father's spiritual advisor. He lives with me at my horse farm."

Chapter 12

THEY CALL IT Kentucky *Bluegrass*, but I have never seen rolling pastures so *green*.

We were making our final approach for a landing at Fort Campbell, Kentucky, home of the 101st Airborne. The lush ground below looked like the world's best-kept golf course.

Special Agent Judge and I had flown from Georgia to Kentucky in an unmarked government jet even though I could've just teleported. Agent Judge, on the other hand? Not so much.

As we were cleared for landing, the FBI special agent once again apologized for his "overzealous subordinates."

"A lot of those guys in the hazmat suits are rookies, Daniel," he explained. "IOU is in a total rebuilding mode. Six months ago, eighty percent of my team was wiped out during an unfortunate encounter with a four-sided killing machine."

"Attila," I said.

"Come again?"

"My nickname for Number 33, the cubist Varladrian warrior your team bumped up against. But don't worry—he won't be giving you guys any more grief."

"Is that right?"

"Yeah. I hear he recently had a heart attack."

Agent Judge's horse farm was a two-hour drive from the Fort Campbell airbase. Ribbons of bright white fencing penned in pastures of emerald green, where magnificent horses lazily nibbled on the grass.

"We have a hundred and thirty-two acres," said Agent Judge as he piloted his Jeep up a long asphalt driveway toward a Victorian-style farmhouse. "The perimeter is secure and patrolled, so don't worry—you'll be safe here, Daniel."

The picturesque farmhouse sat perched on a shady knoll dead ahead, but Agent Judge turned his Jeep toward the open doors of a bright red horse barn.

"Um, isn't Xanthos waiting for us?" I asked.

"Roger that," said Agent Judge. "That's why I thought we'd swing by his place first."

The barn was beautiful. It had those quaint Dutch doors, and a bunch of sliding panels decorated with white X's inside white squares. Looked like the picture-perfect barn from an "Old McDonald" play set. But still...

"You make my father's spiritual advisor live in a *horse barn*?"

Agent Judge brought the Jeep to a stop. "Where else? Xanthos is a horse, Daniel. A champion Thoroughbred."

49

Chapter 13

THE MOST MAGNIFICENT white stallion I had ever seen stood nibbling hay in a pristine stall.

He was a noble steed straight out of a Disney cartoon. Golden sunlight streaming through an open window made his coat and mane shimmer like freshly fallen snow. His bright blue eyes, the same color as mine, sparkled. Every inch of the beautiful beast was white on white on white. Picture vanilla ice cream topped with whipped cream and wispy cotton candy.

Ah, Daniel, the horse said in my mind. *Welcome! It is so, so good to see you once again.*

Now, if *you* ever start hearing horse voices in your head, you should probably call 911 or check in with the school nurse. But I had held telepathic conversations with animals before, including my all-time favorite, Chordata, one of the elephants back home on Alpar Nok.

Hello, Xanthos, I thought back. *I don't remember meeting you before....*

The horse let loose a laugh. It wasn't exactly a high-pitched *horse* laugh. More like a jolly Jamaican chuckle.

Of course you do not remember, Daniel. You were very, very young. Stinky Boy they called you, yah?

Okay. Time out. Does everybody I meet, including barnyard animals, have to remember that particular nickname?

"Um, I'll leave you two alone," said Agent Judge. "It looks like you have a lot to, uh, *talk* about."

Shaking his head, the special agent strolled out of the horse barn.

Poor Agent Judge. He does not understand how we communicate. Xanthos rumbled up another soft chuckle. *You would like to know more about me, yah, mon?*

I nodded.

Very well. I come to Earth from the far, far reaches of the Milky Way, from the planet Pfeerdia, in what your Earth astronomers call the Dark Horse Nebula—a name, I must say, that greatly amuses me.

Xanthos shook out his sleek white mane and flicked his feathery white tail. There was absolutely nothing dark about this horse, unless, of course, you counted his hooves.

My Pfeerdian ancestors were among the first quadrupeds to settle in the Arabian Peninsula.

Of course, I thought. *That's why champion Thoroughbred racehorses all trace their ancestry to Arabian stallions!*

Yah, mon. But when we race against Earth animals, we rein ourselves in. To do otherwise would not be sporting. You see, Daniel, four-legged Pfeerdians can easily trot at one hundred miles per hour.

I was impressed. *Um, what do you guys consider "galloping"?*

When we break the sound barrier, brudda. Heh, heh, heh.

So, I inquired, *why did you come to Earth?*

For Kentucky, Xanthos replied with a contented sigh. *For us, this is heaven. We are treated here like royalty. And the grass? Oh, my, Daniel. It is sooo delicious. Very, very tasty and sweet. I would be so, so sad if anything bad were to befall this beautiful place....*

Xanthos's thoughts drifted off. For the first time since meeting this fellow alien, I sensed a non-mellow vibe. Fear? Dread? Something was definitely upsetting his laid-back mojo.

What is it you are afraid of? I asked.

Much, Daniel. Much. The coming battle. The final struggle. Your mission to take on Number 2.

I needed to clear up that little misconception. *Um, taking out Number 2 won't be the final battle, Xanthos. The Prayer, the most evil alien residing on Earth, is still my primary objective. My mission on Terra Firma won't be complete until I do to him what he did to my family.*

Ah, yes. Revenge. A very powerful, very exhilarating emotion.

I'm not doing this for laughs. That beast killed my parents!

Take care, my yute. Beware of darkness. For in the darkness, it is sometimes difficult to see where the good ends and the evil begins. Do not give sway to the negative way.

Right. I'd almost forgotten: Xanthos was supposed to be

my *spiritual* advisor. Luke Skywalker had Yoda; I got a reggae rocking horse.

Look, I communicated, *first things first. I need to prepare myself to take out Number 2. Can you help me or not?*

Of course, Daniel, of course. You must know this: a red horse shall be a sign.

A sign of what?

Of all that is written, of all that must be.

Gee. Could you be a little more vague? I was starting to question the whole notion of "horse sense" meaning sound and practical. This particular equine specimen kept speaking to me in riddles. *You're my spiritual advisor, right?*

The stallion dipped its head slightly. *That I am, mon.*

Then come on: Advise me! What do I need to do?

Soon, much. For the moment? Chill. Rest and restore your powers. For you will need each and every one of them—now more than ever.

Chapter 14

FOLLOWING DOCTOR'S ORDERS (make that spiritual advisor's orders) meant it was time for some serious R and R — rest and relaxation.

Xanthos was right: If I was going to go up against Number 2, I needed to be tanned, rested, and ready to rock. I needed *all* my powers at my command.

So we went horseback riding.

"Show me what you can do!" I shouted as we cantered across a grassy field.

Xanthos gave me one of his cheery chuckles and hit the gas. Soon we were galloping across a blurred sea of green. We didn't throttle all the way up to Mach One — we didn't want our sonic boom to shatter all the windows up in Agent Judge's farmhouse — but we did move faster than I've ever traveled on the back of any animal, stampeding elephants included.

Would you like to fly? I heard Xanthos ask in my mind.

Visions of Pegasus, the winged horse from Greek mythology, danced through my head. *Can you do that?*

Well, not in front of our human hosts, but yah. Four-legged Pfeerdians are famous for flight.

Try saying *that* four times fast.

"Then," I cried out, "let's do it!"

Grab hold of my mane, mon. Hang on tight.

I gripped his bristly white withers in my fist and, at my signal, we lifted off. It was like I was floating on a carousel (without the corny calliope music, thank you very much), bobbing up and down—only wooden horses can't soar across open fields like a Ferrari in fifth gear.

We were zooming along, maybe three feet off the ground, skimming across the rippling grass like an air-hockey puck tooling along at warp speed. Up ahead, I saw a thicket of trees.

Care to do a little off-roading, Daniel?

Definitely!

Xanthos let out another chuckle and headed for the forest. Now we were zipping through trees and underbrush, ducking under branches, scooting around stumps. Leaves, twigs, pine needles, pinecones, and maybe even a chipmunk or two (sorry about that, Emma) got sucked into the swirling vortex of our wake.

I could see a roaring creek, maybe twenty feet wide, coming up.

"Let's jump it!"

With pleasure, mon.

We reached the bank, bounded up, and sailed above the stream.

Until we weren't flying anymore.

Suddenly Xanthos stalled, tucked in his forelegs, let out a frightened whinny, and belly-flopped into the creek.

My saddle slipped sideways. I slid down his flank with one foot still stuck in a stirrup. Finally kicking free, I fell into the water headfirst—my second water-slide ride in less than twenty-four hours.

Fortunately, the rapids were shallow.

Unfortunately, they were lined with rocks.

But since it was a sweltering-hot summer day, the dunk was actually kind of invigorating—I mean, once I got over the shock of the temperature plunge and the embarrassment of looking like a klutz.

When I came up, soaking wet and sputtering water, I once again heard Xanthos's voice in my head.

Sorry about that, mon. He nudged his muzzle toward the shoreline. *But we have an unexpected observer.*

Chapter 15

UP ON THE creek bank, mounted on a chestnut-brown mare, I saw a very cute girl.

Very, as in *extremely*.

She was wearing jeans, knee-high boots, a snug T-shirt with a cool I RIDE graphic, riding gloves, and one of those velvety black helmets with a button on top. She looked to be my age, and she had fair skin, blond hair (tucked up under the helmet), and the most amazing laugh I had ever heard—even if she was laughing at *me*.

"Ride much?" she said.

"Um, not really."

I sloshed a little closer to the shore, the creek water squishing in my sneakers. I wanted to see if the girl's eyes were really as brilliantly blue as the summer sky. Behind me, Xanthos whinnied and neighed and pawed at the water. My spiritual advisor was putting on a big act, pretending to be a humble horse.

The girl dismounted, came to the shore, shot out her hand, and helped me haul myself out of the creek.

Her eyes? Even bluer than the sky. We're talking sapphires.

"Did you hurt yourself?" she asked, sounding genuinely concerned.

"Not really. Just dented my pride a little, I guess."

"Hey, we all fall off now and then. The trick is being brave enough to climb back on."

I could've given her a cocky grin and bounded back up into the saddle like I had a rocket pack on my back. I could've recited a Shakespearean sonnet, or a few verses from a cheesy Hallmark Valentine's Day card. I could've said or done something super sappy to try to describe the fluttering feeling flipping around in my stomach.

But I didn't.

I just stood there, soaking wet, gazing into the most amazingly awesome eyes I had ever gazed, gawked, or gaped into. Eyes more incredible than Dana's, and Dana is, quite literally, the girl of my dreams.

Dana.

That's exactly who this girl on the horse reminded me of. Only she wasn't a product of my imagination! This girl, as far as I could tell, was real.

Oh, yes, Daniel—she is quite real, I heard Xanthos say in my head. *Her name is Mel, short for Melody, a name that suits her personality quite well, yah? She is like the song you hear in the morning and cannot get out of your head all day. Heh, heh, heh.*

This time, I chuckled along with my spiritual advisor.

She is also Agent Judge's daughter.

I grinned.

You were right about Kentucky, I thought back to Xanthos. *It is extremely heavenly, mon.*

Chapter 16

TURNS OUT I wasn't the first alien Mel had ever met.

"One time, Dad brought home this super-friendly turtle-type thingy."

We were walking along a bridle path, leading our horses by their reins. Butterflies were flitting all around—or maybe that was just in my stomach.

"Her name was Jenn Jenn," said Mel.

"The turtle-type thingy?"

She laughed. "Well, that's what she looked like. She was in the witness protection program or something. I think Jenn Jenn was helping my dad track down an alien he kept calling 'Number 5.'"

I nodded. I had met the fifth-foulest fiend on the planet. I had also terminated him.

"Anyway," said Mel, "Jenn Jenn and I hung out for a couple weeks. She was wicked good at chess. And you did *not* want to watch *Jeopardy!* with her, because Jenn Jenn knew all the questions before Alex Trebek even finished reading the answers!"

I nodded. "Probably from Sulleean. Super-intelligent creatures. They're basically a big brain wobbling around on four feet, with a tiny head that pokes out when they need to eat or scan something."

"Or play *Jeopardy!*," added Mel.

"Right. That tortoiseshell? It's actually an exoskeletal skull."

"Really? Wow. It sure was cool-looking. Swirly, luminous colors, like on a bowling ball. Do you guys have bowling up on Alpar Nok?"

"We have something similar. But you need a zero-gravity playing field, suborbital meteorites, and an asteroid belt."

"Really? Do you wear the belt?"

"No, an asteroid belt is—"

She poked me in the ribs with her elbow. "Kidding!"

I smiled. She smiled. Yes, it was an official smilefest.

"So," said Mel, "seeing how you're already soaked, you want to hit my favorite swimming hole? It's up that dirt road a couple miles. We could ride there."

"Is it on your property?"

"No. Our neighbor's. But they don't mind. I swim there all the time."

Do not stray outside the secure perimeter, said a small voice inside my head, and this time it wasn't Xanthos, although he did chime in with a *Yah, mon. Very, very bad idea. Do not go looking for trouble. You will find it soon enough.*

I had to agree with Dr. X, which is what I had decided to call Xanthos since he was quickly becoming my built-in Dr. Phil, constantly dispensing pearls of wisdom and loads of tough love. I knew that Number 2 and his hench-thugs from the bat cave were still out there, still passing around my WANTED poster, still gunning for me. And if Mel happened to be with me when some alien bounty hunter finally tracked me down, the creep would not discriminate. It would blast her to smithereens, too.

Yes, I needed to rest and restore my powers.

But I did not need to be stupid.

"I have a better idea," I said.

"What?"

"You ever ride an elephant?"

Chapter 17

"THAT. WAS. SO. *Amazing!*"

With Dr. X's permission, I had just transformed both of our horses into giant pachyderms.

"How did you do that?"

I gave Mel the standard magician's answer: "Quite well, don't you think?"

"No, really, Daniel. Where did these elephants come from?"

I shrugged. "My imagination."

"Wow. Einstein was so totally right!"

"Huh?"

"Albert Einstein. Frizzy hair? Genius? E equals mc squared?"

I nodded. I knew the guy. I had even proven several of his theories, like that one where he said, "The separation between past, present, and future is only an illusion, although a convincing one." That was *so* true.

"Oh, by the way," said Mel, "was Einstein an alien, too?"

"Sorry," I said with a grin. "I am not at liberty to divulge that information."

"Well, anyway, Einstein said, 'Imagination is more important than knowledge.'"

I went ahead and finished the rest of the quote: "'For knowledge is limited to all we now know and understand, while imagination embraces the entire world, and all there ever will be to know and understand.'"

"Exactly," said Mel. "So, can you create anything you dream up?"

"I guess. But I have to grok it first."

"Oh, like in *Stranger in a Strange Land*?" said Mel.

"You've read Robert A. Heinlein's book?"

"Well, duh," said Mel. "Hasn't everybody?"

"Well..."

"To grok is to understand something so thoroughly that the observer becomes part of the observed! It's like you totally drink it in!"

We continued our discussion of grokking, and Alpar Nok, and whether Justin Bieber was an alien as we plodded across the rolling fields, swaying in the basket seats on the backs of our giant elephants (I had supersized our mastodons because they're even cooler to ride when they're the size of massive woolly mammoths). Even Dr. X was enjoying the ride.

I have always wanted to walk a mile in my brudda's hooves, he said in my head. *Thank you, Daniel, for making it possible.*

You're welcome, brudda, I thought back, aping his reg-

gae slang for "brother." *But are you a hundred percent certain this is what I need to be doing right now? I'm extremely
worried about Number 2.*

What are you so worried about?

*That I won't be ready to take him down when this battle
you keep talking about finally takes place. I don't even know
who or what I'm up against. The List draws a total blank on
his powers, his planet of origin, his —*

*Worry is wasted energy, Daniel. It is like praying for
things you don't really want.*

But...

This is very important, your time with Mel.

How?

*You are experiencing humanity at its best. Joy. Friendship.
Perhaps even the first inklings of love, yah?*

*Whoa, ease up, Dr. X. Hold your horses. This is our first
date and, technically, it's not even a date. It's just a horse ride
that, you know, turned into an elephant ride.*

*Heh, heh, heh. Savor this moment, Daniel. Drink it in and,
as you say, grok it. For the time is coming when hate will seem
to conquer love. And Daniel?*

Yes?

You must not let the darkness win!

Chapter 18

"SO, DANIEL," MEL said after I turned our elephants back into horses. "What's next?"

Mel was radiant. Happiness filled her face. To tell the truth, I was feeling pretty giddy, too.

"I dunno," I said. "What do you want to do?"

"I dunno. Hey—there's this really cool cave up at the base of that hill. We could go in there, and you could turn the bats into flying dinosaurs or something, and the horses could be like brontosauruses...."

Great, I thought. *Another bat cave.*

"Or we could eat," said Joe as he climbed over the white fence behind the horse barn, followed by Emma, Willy, and, of course, Dana.

Yes, I had conjured up my four friends.

You know what it's like when you meet somebody who you think is pretty great: you want to make sure your old friends like your new friend as much as you do. Plus, having the gang around meant I could avoid Mel's spelunking idea. What can I say? I'd already fulfilled my subterranean adventure quota for the year.

"Mel," I said, "these are my best friends: Joe, Willy, his sister, Emma—"

"I love your horses, you guys!" Emma gushed as she rushed over to stroke their manes. "Can I feed them an apple?"

"Sure," said Mel.

"Um, Daniel?"

"Yes, Emma?"

"Apples?"

"Coming right up." I snapped my fingers and materialized Emma a bushel full of Granny Smiths, Macintoshes, Braeburns, and Galas—with a couple of carrot stalks and sugar cubes stuffed in down the sides to make it a gourmet gift basket.

"So, Daniel," said Dana, "aren't you going to introduce me to your new...*friend*?"

Okay, this was going to be a wee bit awkward.

How does a guy introduce his dream girl to the girl of his dreams—or vice versa?

Dr. X? I mentally checked in with my trusted steed and advisor.

But all he did was chuckle. *Heh, heh, heh.*

I had to handle this one all by myself.

Welcome to the joys of being a teenage boy.

Chapter 19

WHILE MEL AND Emma fed apples to the horses and Joe and Willy brushed them down, Dana and I slipped away to have A Conversation.

I hate Conversations.

"Come on, Dana. Go easy on Mel. She's nice."

"Oh, yes. She's swell."

"Wait a second," I said. "Are you jealous?"

"Of course. *NOT!*"

Fortunately, Joe came to my rescue.

"I'm starving," he said. "Where's the nearest Kentucky Fried Chicken?"

Mel heard that and laughed.

"What?" said Joe. "This is Kentucky, is it not?"

"We don't eat fried chicken every day," said Mel.

"No chicken for me," said Emma. "I don't eat anything with a face."

The six of us swept into the kitchen through the back

door and I was all set to materialize our finger-lickin' good feast when Agent Judge stormed into the room.

"You need to see this, Daniel. *Now.*"

He snapped on an under-the-counter TV set. A horrific news report from Washington, D.C., filled the screen.

The time for R and R was officially over.

As I watched I was sickened by the image of the gleaming marble sides of the Washington Monument appearing to crackle with spidery fissure lines, like a shattering sheet of ice.

Giant marble slabs slid down the sides of the obelisk, like the walls of a crumbling glacier. The deafening roar of the thunderous rockslide rumbled across Washington, D.C., as Number 2 brought down the world's tallest stone structure. Five hundred and fifty-five feet of marble, granite, and sandstone crumbled before his glowering red eyes, sending up a billowing cloud of dust and destruction that blotted out the sun and darkened the sky.

As if this weren't sickening enough, I heard a voice from the newscast that was all too familiar. And it was talking to me.

"See this and know who I am, Daniel X!" Number 2 whispered, unfurling his enormous black wings. "This is all for you!"

Chapter 20

IT WAS THE Fourth of July, and the second-deadliest alien in the universe was enjoying the most spectacular "fireworks" display the nation's capital had ever seen.

He had already torched the White House, charring its ruins black.

He had laid waste to the Lincoln Memorial, rolling the sainted president's sculpted head into a rat-infested sewer.

He had crushed the Capitol Building, flattening its Great Rotunda as if the cast-iron dome were nothing more than an aluminum Coke can.

Meanwhile, his alien army was sweeping like a plague of locusts across the metropolitan area to usher survivors down into the abyss.

His name was Abbadon.

Hoping to enslave millions, he quickly assumed the guise of a concerned newscaster and infiltrated the earthlings' television broadcasts, as well as their Internet, cell phones, and encrypted National Security networks. His face filled video screens everywhere.

"People of Washington, D.C., if you wish to live, flee your homes and join me underground. The world as you have known it is nearing its apocalyptic end. Come to me and survive. Refuse me and die."

Everywhere, flecks of debris drifted down from the ominous sky like mammoth gray snowflakes. Those who wished to survive stampeded toward the underground entrances to Washington's Metro system, where Abbadon had stationed his minions, all of whom, as had been decreed ages ago, now appeared with locust wings and scorpion tails.

As more monuments and landmarks and office towers collapsed, riots erupted among those clawing their way toward the subway entrances. A few of the greediest humans took advantage of the chaos and leaped through shattered shop windows to loot the shelves.

Two brothers fought each other over the last loaf of bread in a convenience store. Abbadon reveled in the sight. He delighted in the depraved indifference these terrified creatures now showed to those they had once considered their fellow men.

Now it was every man and woman for him- or herself.

The human animals were viciously turning on one another in their Darwinian pursuit of survival.

All is as it was always meant to be, thought Abbadon. *My time is at hand!*

Chapter 21

I COULD NOT believe my eyes.

Washington, D.C., looked worse than it did in the movie *Independence Day*.

All across the capital, buildings were imploding—coming down on themselves and sending up swirling clouds of dust and debris.

Happy Fourth of July, everybody.

This had to be Number 2's doing; Washington had been the first city mentioned on his hit list back in the bat cave.

"We need to be there," I said to Agent Judge. "Now."

"A chopper is on the way. It'll ferry us down to Fort Campbell, where we can hitch a ride on a C-140 transport plane. They've already loaded IOU's ATV into the cargo hold."

"With all due respect, Agent Judge," I said, "we're going to need a whole lot more than an all-terrain vehicle to go up against the universe's second-most-vicious alien outlaw."

"It's an Alien Tracking Vehicle, Daniel."

"Still, I'd rather—"

"Your father designed it for us. We still don't know what half the gizmos and gadgets inside the thing do."

"Don't worry," said Joe, my own personal Geek Squad. "I'll figure it out."

"We need to hustle," said Willy. "Check out the creepy-crawlers Number 2's found to do his dirty work."

CNN was airing live footage of Number 2's insect-like minions herding terrified citizens toward the entrances to D.C.'s underground Metro system. The beasts appeared to be about seven feet tall, with curled tails, see-through locust wings, and hideous human heads. They used their pointed tails as cattle prods to drive the hordes of humans down steep staircases and into the subway tunnels.

"Wait a second," I said. "What do we know about their weaponry? How did Number 2 bring down all those buildings?"

Special Agent Judge consulted a handheld computer that was feeding him real-time updates from the Federal Bureau of Investigation's former headquarters in downtown D.C. I say "former" because the J. Edgar Hoover Building, a massive structure made out of raw concrete poured over steel beams, was now a pile of chunky gray gravel on Pennsylvania Avenue, just a few blocks east of what used to be the White House.

"My guys on the streets report seeing no incoming missiles, no blasts from orbiting spacecraft, nothing," said Agent Judge.

"No way," said Dana. "That's impossible."

"He must've used stealth weaponry of some sort," said Willy, our intergalactic arms expert.

That's when I remembered the laser-beam blasts Number 2 used to throw the hench-lackeys who had dared to laugh during his underground pep rally.

"I saw Number 2 take out a couple of his goons back in that cavern just by glaring at them. His eyes are like high-energy laser beams."

Maybe when he took down the class clowns, he had his eyeballs set on Stun like they used to do on *Star Trek*. Then, once he arrived in Washington, he'd flicked his high beams up to Total Devastation.

"Have we heard anything about casualties?" I asked Agent Judge.

"Affirmative. There aren't any."

"*What?* That's impossible. I just saw —"

"So far, no one's been killed or injured. Number 2 is destroying the entire city, but not the citizens."

"So," said Willy, "whatever he's using, it's the complete opposite of a neutron bomb. Instead of killing all the people and saving the infrastructure, he's wiping out the structures while sparing the civilians."

"This makes no sense," I mumbled. "None of it."

"There's only one way for us to figure out what's really going on," said Mel. "We need to be in D.C. Now!"

"Us?" said Dana, arching an eyebrow. "We?"

"What? You don't seriously think I'm going to hang here while the country I love is under attack?"

"Now, Mel," said Agent Judge, "we've talked about this before. It isn't safe out there."

"Dad!" Mel exclaimed, gesturing at the TV screen. "I don't think *any* place on Earth is safe right now."

"You can't come," I said to Mel. "I've made a vow to never risk human life when dealing with alien outlaws on Terra Firma."

"Really?" said Mel with a crooked smile. "Well, Daniel, I've made a vow, too: to never be a wimp. So come on. Like you said, we need to be in D.C.!"

Chapter 22

IT WAS DUSK when we finally rolled into the Virginia suburbs just west of the capital.

My dad had done an amazingly awesome job outfitting the Alien Tracker Vehicle for the FBI. Joe was practically drooling as he fiddled with all the sensor knobs and sliders arrayed across the control panel in the back of the sleek, aerodynamic truck. The van's speedometer topped out at 288 mph (my dad had obviously tweaked out the engine, too), which, of course, was the equivalent to 250 knots, the maximum speed an aircraft can fly below 10,000 feet.

Yep. I wouldn't be surprised if pretty soon Joe found a toggle switch that deployed wings on both sides of the titanium truck.

"Do we have weapons?" asked Agent Judge, who was up front, riding shotgun, while one of his top IOU guys manned the wheel and piloted the vehicle through the smoldering ruins of Arlington, Virginia.

"Definitely," said Joe. "Blaster cannons, stun guns, and an extremely lethal rotating rocket launcher up on the roof."

"But we won't use any of the weapons unless we absolutely, positively have to, right, Daniel?" said Emma, who, of course, was wearing her Birkenstocks and GIVE PEACE A CHANCE T-shirt.

"Of course we won't use any weapons," sniped Dana. "We'll just very politely ask these scorpion-tailed locust scuzzballs to put everything back the way they found it."

"That won't work," fumed Willy, who was standing up, bracing himself against the bulkhead between the front of the truck and the crew area. Dana rolled her eyes.

The ATV bounded over potholes and rubble as we passed what was left of the Iwo Jima Memorial (the flag lay in tatters atop a mound of melted bronze). The driver was heading for the Arlington Memorial Bridge.

A dozen plasma-screen TVs mounted on the interior walls of the ATV displayed images of the mass destruction awaiting us when we crossed the Potomac River to enter the District of Columbia.

"There's nothing left," Mel announced with a gasp. "I came here on a class trip last spring...the cherry blossoms were in bloom...."

Now there wasn't a tree of any kind standing anywhere.

Or a monument. Or a building. Not even a mailbox or parking meter.

Mel was seated next to me on the crew bench. I squeezed her hand, hard.

Because the images of devastation playing out on the video monitors were tearing me apart.

Hey, I'm a guy blessed with the greatest superpower of them all: the ability to *create* anything I can grok in my imagination. As a *creator*, nothing breaks my heart more than this kind of mass *destruction*. An entire city laid to waste. Magnificent monuments to everything my adopted home stands for, reduced to rubble. And yes, like Mel, I thought the National Cherry Blossom Festival—held in early April, when the Yoshino, Akebono, Usuzumi, and Fugenzo blooms hit their peak—was as stunningly beautiful as anything on any planet anywhere. And next spring? It just wouldn't happen.

If there even was a next spring.

"Heads up," said the driver. "We have company."

I swiveled in my seat and looked out the front window.

I wished I hadn't.

Chapter 23

AS WE ENTERED Washington from the west, a crazed swarm of people, numbering in the thousands, came charging across the arched bridge, headed for Virginia.

Our driver slammed on the brakes. The mob parted and swept around the ATV, surrounding us like a raging river ready to overrun its banks.

"There's a Metro station on the other side of the bridge, back in Arlington!" said Agent Judge. "That's where they're all headed."

As the crowd swarmed around our vehicle, I checked out the video monitors. Some showed terrified residents of D.C. trampling one another like there was a day-after-Thanksgiving door-buster sale going on down in the subway stations. Others showed Number 2's wing-backed goons pillaging and plundering across the wasteland that had once been the capital city of the most powerful nation on Earth.

One of the locust-like creatures had found himself a

Ferrari and was cutting tire-screeching, rubber-burning doughnuts inside the drained concrete basin of the Lincoln Memorial reflecting pool.

Some other beasts were outside the Library of Congress, burning all the books.

A trio of thugs standing on the broken steps of the crumpled Capitol tucked in their scorpion tails and smiled so they could satellite-beam souvenir images of themselves back to friends on their home planets.

Just then, an air horn blared a warning.

A battery of red LEDs flashed across Joe's control board.

"We've got aliens," he said. "Sensors are picking them up at less than one hundred meters away."

"Get ready to rumble," said Willy.

"I see them!" Mel said, pointing toward the windshield.

In the distance, swinging down the line of cast-iron lampposts lining both sides of the Arlington Memorial Bridge, I could see four of Number 2's locust-winged, scorpion-tailed alien enforcers.

"There's no exit!" shouted Agent Judge from up front. "We can't leave the truck until this crowd thins out. All doors and points of egress are currently blocked."

I thought about making the van disappear—that'd be one way to get outside, where the action was. But without the vehicle's protective armored shell, we'd be trampled. And Mel, her dad, and the driver couldn't turn themselves into a patch of asphalt and lie down till the stampede passed us over, like I could.

"Joe?" I said. "We need to be outside."

"No problem." He flipped a switch and jabbed his thumb up toward the ceiling. "Roof hatch."

I was on top of the truck first. Willy, my trusted wing-man, hauled himself out of the hatch right behind me. Dana, Emma, and Joe piled out after Willy.

"*She* wants to come out to play, too," reported Dana, nodding down at Mel, who was halfway up the ladder rungs.

"Stay back on this one, Mel," I shouted down into the hole.

"No way. I told you, Daniel: I am not a wimp."

I didn't have time to discuss the matter.

Using simple telekinesis, I slammed down the hatch lid and spun its wheel lock tight. Then, sparks flying, I imagined the cap being sealed with a thin bead of iron made molten under the blinding arc of an acetylene torch.

"Nice spot welding," said Joe.

"Thanks."

"Now," said Willy, "can we finally go take care of this plague of scorpion-tailed locust losers?"

Chapter 24

I LEAPED OFF the roof of the ATV and landed forty-some feet away, on the narrow ledge of the bridge's guardrail.

"I've got your back!" shouted Emma, who was right behind me.

With the Potomac River on our left, the screaming horde on our right, and the sky going dark up above, it felt like we were walking the plank—*blindfolded*.

"We've got these two scuzzbuckets," yelled Willy. He was on the far side of the bridge, racing down the other guard-rail. Dana and Joe were tearing up the beam behind him.

The trio was aiming for a pair of the giant creatures who were using their muscular grasshopper-style legs to bound toward Virginia. When the hideous aliens reached a pair of mammoth pedestals, they skittered up the stone bases to stand beside two seventeen-foot-tall American eagle statues.

"Hurry!" one of the goons growled from its perch to the mob below. "Meet your Lord and Master down below!"

Emma and I had the other two supersized vermin waiting for us atop the forty-foot-tall pedestals on our side of the bridge.

"Daniel?" Emma called as we charged single-file down the granite banister as if we were competing in a new Olympic sport: Balance Beam Wind Sprints.

"Yeah?"

"We can neutralize these things without killing them, right?"

If there were a Society for the Prevention of Cruelty to Insects, Emma would definitely be a charter member. Maybe president.

"We can try," I said as I leaped up into the air. Shooting out a leg, I aimed my foot at what looked like one of the gangly creature's knees or upper ankles. Emma came off the stone slab as if it were a trampoline, soared up the side of the pedestal, and grabbed hold of the second brute's flapping foot.

Since we had opted for empty-hand combat, Emma was attempting to trip up her bad dude and dunk him down into the Potomac. I, on the other hand, was hypothesizing that my alien's skinny kneecap would be brittle enough to break when I drop-kicked it at super-high velocity.

It wasn't.

Sure, it crunched the way bugs do when you step on them, but it didn't snap.

"Daniel!" I heard Emma scream. Her attack plan wasn't working, either. The beast shook her off its foot like she was a wad of chewing gum stuck to the bottom of its tennis shoe. Emma was now the one plummeting down toward the river.

Fortunately, she was able to hook the guardrail with her fingernails just before she plunged past it.

Unfortunately, my failed flying karate kick had infuriated my bony-kneed target. The thing howled and swiped at me with two or three of its fuzz-fringed arms. I bounded backward off the lip of the pedestal, tumbled down forty feet, and nailed my one-foot-in-front-of-the-other landing on the guardrail just in time to grab Emma before she lost her grip.

Over on the other side of the bridge, things were even worse.

Chapter 25

LOCUST MAN 3 had Willy locked in all four of its grue-some clutches and was holding him as if he were an ice-cream cone to be licked with a tongue oozing saliva the consistency of corn syrup.

Meanwhile, Joe was stuck under the same freak's floppy black foot.

"We need weapons," I heard Willy shout through the thing's sticky slurps.

Ninety feet away from the action, I quickly material-ized an FDNY fireboat pump and hose so I could water-cannon the creepazoid with thirty-eight thousand gallons of Potomac River water per minute. The gusher smacked the thing in its thorax with a wet *SPLAT!* Luckily, as it began to topple off the pedestal and into the river, it dropped Willy and Joe was able to roll free. The two of them raced back toward the truck to grab the rocket launcher off the roof.

Why didn't they ask me to quickly materialize some instant weaponry?

Easy: they knew I'd be busy.

The fourth locust-scorpion thing had *Dana* in its grip.

"Daniel?" she shouted. "*Now* would be an excellent time to turn yourself into an electric bug zapper!"

I zoomed across the span of the bridge, hurdling over the heads of the stragglers who were bringing up the rear of the crowd racing for the subway entrance in Virginia. Above me, the monster started whirling its wings. It lifted off from the eagle pedestal like a turbocharged helicopter, hauling Dana straight up to fifty, sixty, maybe a hundred feet above the bridge.

"Hang on!" I shouted up to the starry sky, where all I could make out was the squirming silhouette of Dana in the grip of the giant flying insect. I scurried up the pedestal and was about to turn myself into a Black-winged Pratincole (an African bird that *loves* to hawk for locusts) when I heard a deafening screech.

"*Eeeeee!*"

It sounded exactly like the squeal a lobster makes when you plop it into a pot of boiling water.

Then I heard three more ear-piercing wails.

"*Eeeeeeeee!*"

Up above, the flying fiend's claws snapped open.

Dana fell from the sky.

So did the giant locust.

Darting sideways, I caught Dana right before she impaled herself on the very sharp tip of a sculpted eagle wing.

"We've got the rocket launcher!" Willy shouted as he and Joe raced up the bridge lugging what looked like an extremely heavy, multi-barreled Gatling gun.

The bug I had blasted off its pedestal into the river used two of its appendages to climb up over the side of the short bridge. The other two limbs were holding the sides of its head as it screamed in unrelenting pain.

Back on the other side, the two aliens who had been harassing Emma were grabbing what appeared to be ear-holes in their vaguely humanoid heads. They were also wailing.

"Eeeeeee!"

The baddie that had nabbed Dana lay on its back in the middle of the asphalt roadway, shrieking and kicking its feet.

"Eeeeeeeee!"

Now the other three beasts toppled to the ground, twitching their hideous, sawtooth-ridged legs in the air as they cried out in agony.

"Eeeeeeeee!"

Then all four of the creatures stopped squealing.

They went totally stiff.

From my perch up on the northern pedestal, I felt like I was looking down on the giant set of a Raid commercial.

"Are they dead?" asked Dana, who was still nestled in my arms.

"Looks like it," I said.

Cradled against my chest, Dana leaned up and startled me with a kiss.

"You're still my hero," she whispered softly. "Even if you do have a weird thing for Earth girls."

"Come on, Dana. Mel's nice. She's also *real*."

"Whatever. I'm just happy to be alive, even if it's only in your imagination."

"That was awesome, Daniel," said Joe, after I had carried Dana down to the roadway to join the rest of the gang.

Yes, Dana could've jumped down on her own, but I got the feeling she liked being back in my arms.

To tell the truth, I didn't mind it, either.

"So," asked Willy, "how'd you take down all four bogies at the same time?"

I shrugged. "I didn't."

Dana put a hand on her hip. Shot me her "give me a break" eyes.

"Well, if you didn't do it," asked Emma, "who did?"

"Hey, you guys — were those four the only troublemakers?"

It was Mel. Her voice was booming out of a loudspeaker mounted on top of the FBI truck.

"Or are there more locusts for me to eliminate from this equation?"

Chapter 26

"THERE'S A TOWN in Kentucky called Locust," Mel informed us as the ATV, with all of us back inside, crawled through the deserted streets of what used to be Washington, D.C. Now it looked like something out of the Stone Age.

"So," she continued, "we know how to deal with the noisy little buggers when they swarm into town to devour our crops."

"So what'd you do?" asked Willy. "Blast them with some kind of invisible insect-repellent death ray?"

Mel smiled her crooked grin—the one that had totally stopped my heart when she'd flashed it at me as I came out of that creek soaking wet.

"Something like that," she said. "I rigged up the van's sound system to act as an ultrasonic device and blasted extremely high-frequency waves out of the external speakers, because locusts have complex tympanic organs...."

"Huh?" said Joe.

Emma helped him out. "Ears, basically. A stretched membrane backed by an air sac and sensory neurons. Sort of like a tiny tympani drum with nerves."

"Oh," said Joe. "Eardrums."

"We humans can't hear sounds pitched higher than twenty thousand hertz," Mel continued, "but locusts can detect frequencies up to *one hundred thousand* hertz."

"They teach you this at horse school, Mel?" Dana said, somewhat snidely.

"Nope. Middle school."

"Uh-oh," Joe said, gesturing toward the monitor mounted above the truck's blinking control panel. "Here comes something else humans are gonna wish they couldn't hear."

He amped up the master volume knob, and we heard the final trumpet strains of "Hail to the Chief."

Every flat-screen TV was now filled with the official seal of the President of the United States.

"Pull over," Agent Judge said to the driver. "We probably need to watch this. Looks like President McManus has activated the Emergency Broadcast System."

The driver crunched over to what remained of the curb. According to a sign I saw lying in the wreckage, we were on Constitution Avenue, right in front of the ruins of the National Archives Building, which had once looked like the Parthenon in Athens.

Now it looked more or less like the scrap pile behind Granite 'R' Us.

"Here we go," said Willy as the presidential seal faded away.

A very nervous President John McManus—who hailed from Tennessee and had snowy-white hair—sat behind a military-issue steel desk with his hands folded, trying to look calm and presidential. There were no American flags on the desk, no family photographs.

"He must be in the bunker," said Agent Judge. "The secure underground location where they'd take the president if we ever had a nuclear attack."

"Ladies and gentlemen," cooed an off-camera voice, which I immediately recognized as belonging to Number 2, "the President of the United States."

"My fellow Americans," said President McManus, "I come to you this evening with a heavy heart. For many years, we, your leaders in the United States government, have dreaded the day when alien beings from planets unknown would land on Earth and, with their superior weaponry, conquer us. Well, as you have undoubtedly heard, that day has arrived. Today, our nation's capital was taken over by an invading army of technologically advanced alien invaders."

"What?" said Willy. "He's already surrendered?"

"Sure sounds like it," said Joe.

"To those of you currently residing outside of Washington, D.C., be advised: your own Armageddon is rapidly approaching."

"Tomorrow," said the off-screen voice.

"That voice. That's him, right, Daniel?" said Mel. "Number 2?"

"Yeah."

The camera pushed in tighter on the president's very

worried face. "My fellow Americans, I urge you all to lay down your weapons. Do not fight back. Our victorious visitors have promised me that no American citizens will be harmed as long as we all do as we are told."

"Man," said Willy, "how much mistletoe is hanging off Number 2's coattails? The president is kissing his butt, big-time."

"This is bad," said Emma. "I mean, I'm all for *peace*, but not without justice...."

Me? I figured it was the same-old, same-old:

Politicians selling their souls to the highest bidder.

Chapter 27

"IN CONCLUSION," SAID President McManus, "rest assured that the government of the United States is still quite functional, here in our secure underground facility."

The camera widened out to show a cluster of very important-looking men and women in business suits, plus a couple of guys in military uniforms.

"The Speaker of the House, the vice president, the secretaries of state and defense, the Joint Chiefs of Staff, and the Supreme Court agree that it is in our nation's best interest for all of you to surrender peaceably and seek safety in the vast network of shelters our conquerors have established underground."

"Number 2 is a slaver," blurted Emma.

"Maybe that's why there haven't been any casualties," added Agent Judge.

"Right," said Mel. "He doesn't want to *kill* humans; he wants to sell them into slavery!"

"He probably sails around the galaxy, enslaving entire

planets," said Dana. "When he has a fresh load of laborers, he holds an interstellar auction and ships the slaves off to the highest bidder!"

Yes, sick as it may sound, there are still some planets—particularly mining colonies and farming worlds—where slavery not only exists but thrives as it did on this planet from the time of Hammurabi's Code (around 1760 BC) until 1981, when the country of Mauritania became the last nation on Earth to finally outlaw the twisted system.

And, for the record, intergalactic slaves fare no better than those formerly oppressed on Earth. They are forced to do hard labor against their will; their children become their master's property the instant they're born, and can be sold or traded at his whim; and if a slave tries to escape, he or she can be killed.

Number 2 most likely had a fleet of interstellar slaving ships orbiting Earth, waiting for his cargo. Once he rounded up as many humans as he could trap in his subterranean holding pens, he'd sell them to the land barons and mining moguls up on Cordood Three, Drangovan, Bresbilzon, and a dozen other bleak planets where the workers toil from sunup to sundown (which, on Cordood Three, can last seventy-nine hours).

"Remember," said President McManus, "to paraphrase the poet Shakespeare, 'Discretion is the better part of valor.'"

"Everybody always quotes that line," said Mel, "but they leave out the fact that Shakespeare had a big fat *coward* named Falstaff say it!"

"Not to mention the fact that he's quoting it backward," added Emma. "It's 'the better part of valor is discretion.'"

"It is far better to be prudent," the president continued, "than merely courageous. Caution is preferable to rash bravery. Slavery is preferable to death."

Willy shook his head. "So much for the land of the free and the home of the brave."

"He doesn't speak for all of us," said Agent Judge.

"We're not surrendering, right, Dad?" said Mel.

"Well," said Agent Judge, "to quote another Brit, Sir Winston Churchill: 'Never give in, never, never, never, never.'"

"Too bad this Churchill guy isn't president," said Willy.

"He's dead," said Dana.

"So? Even dead, he'd be better than this white-haired yellow belly."

Now the camera swung off President McManus to frame the hideous image of Number 2 himself, standing in the wings.

The massive beast wasn't wearing his custom-tailored Savile Row business suit or smiling newscaster face anymore. He was back in terrifying demon mode, his red eyes burning brightly.

"Good citizens," Number 2 said calmly, "I urge you to hurry. We don't have room down below for *everybody*. When my shelters are full, we will be forced to barricade the entryways and eradicate any stragglers. Oh. One more thing. President McManus?"

The camera swung back to the politician who used to be the most powerful man on Earth.

"Yes, thank you. Our new Lord and Master has advised me that there is one resident of the United States that he is particularly interested in meeting down below. In fact, if this young man will do the right thing, well, Number 2 has given me his word that he will be more inclined to show mercy to those of us currently under his protection."

Every eye in the van was staring at me.

The president leaned forward.

"Daniel?" he said. "If you're out there, son, do the right thing. Turn yourself in. Surrender!"

I guess Number 2 had cut a deal with America's ruling elite: give me Daniel X, and you guys get off easy. Maybe he promised them indoor work on Cordood Three.

Now the president's image was replaced by my pimply yearbook mug shot, the same one Number 2 had shown to his minions down in that sweltering cavern.

According to the text scrolling across the bottom of the screen, I was an "illegal alien" and my capture would earn the captor "Special Work Condition Consideration."

Great.

Now Number 2 had turned the *entire nation* into bounty hunters!

Chapter 28

I WAS USED to being a bad guy to the bad guys, but not a bad guy to the good guys. This was a little too much to absorb.

"Okay, everybody," I said. "Answer me this: If Number 2 is an intergalactic slaver, why does he want *me* more than any other creature currently residing on planet Earth?"

"Easy," said Joe. "You'd be the most awesome slave ever! You could build the pharaoh his pyramids in a heartbeat, just by thinking about them."

"Maybe..."

Once again, all the TV screens were filled with images of citizens fleeing their homes for the so-called safety of the subway tunnels.

"Well, Dad," said Mel, "guess you, me, and Agent Williams are the only humans *not* doing what our president just told us to do."

Agent Judge shook his head. "This isn't the America I remember."

"These colors don't run," mumbled Agent Williams, sitting behind the steering wheel.

I turned to my four friends. "Guys, take five."

"What?" said Dana. "You're not sending us away *again*, are you?"

"These colors don't run, either," said Willy, slapping his hand over his heart.

"I know, Willy. But I need some time to focus. And to run a quick errand."

I blinked and my four best friends in the universe disappeared.

"It's a lot easier to concentrate," I explained, "when I don't have to simultaneously imagineer their existence."

"Of course," said Mel.

"Wait here, you guys," I said as I yanked open a side door. "I'll just be a second."

"Where are you going?" asked Agent Judge, his voice full of fatherly concern.

"To run that errand and, hopefully, find the America we all remember." I head-gestured toward the wreckage of what had once been the nation's temple of freedom.

"Out there?" said Mel.

"Yeah. The rotunda of the National Archives Building. That's where they kept the original, signed copies of the Declaration of Independence, the United States Constitution, and the Bill of Rights. I need to go grab all three because, if you ask me, this country's leaders need to reread its charters of freedom!"

Chapter 29

I CRAWLED THROUGH the wreckage toward the spot where the pin on the Google map in my brain indicated I'd find the National Archives Building's rotunda, thanks to the neuron-based, high-speed Wi-Fi connection in my Alpar Nokian cerebellum.

As I moved forward, I remembered Xanthos's advice: *Beware of darkness.* Right now, I was having some extremely dark thoughts about President McManus and his cowardly cronies—and not just because they'd just put a bounty on my head.

I was ticked off because they'd forgotten what America was supposed to be all about. As a former, much braver president once said, "America is a shining city upon a hill whose beacon light guides freedom-loving people everywhere." I needed to find that shining beacon's three instruction manuals: the Constitution, the Bill of Rights, and the Declaration of Independence.

When I reached the spot where the Charters of

Freedom exhibit stood when the National Archives Building wasn't a scrap heap of neoclassical rubble, I opened my eyes and switched on my handy X-ray vision.

I used it to visually pierce the fallen ceiling slabs, felled columns, and pulverized plaster that made it look like a tour group had arrived here on a bulldozer instead of a bus.

Buried beneath a heap of twisted rebar and chunks of marble was the four-paneled, gold-framed display case holding the four pages of the original United States Constitution, handwritten back in 1787. After quickly levitating a landfill's worth of building debris, I unburied the pen-and-ink version of the United States Constitution.

I peered through the first shattered pane of glass and read the preamble on the yellowed sheets of crisp parchment, filled with loopy calligraphy: "We the people of the United States, in Order to form a more perfect Union, establish Justice, insure domestic Tranquility, provide for the common defense, promote the general Welfare, and secure the Blessings of Liberty to ourselves and our Posterity, do ordain and establish this Constitution for the United States of America."

Okay, so usually government documents—junk like tax forms and change-of-address cards from the post office—don't choke me up. But this? This was the blueprint for running a country based on the premise that all human beings were created equal, that they had the right to life, liberty, and the pursuit of happiness.

Now the Constitution, and all that it stood for, lay trampled on the ground.

And if its brittle, antique parchment was exposed to the elements much longer (Number 2 had ripped off the building's rotunda like the pop-top lid of a Pringles can), the document, like the ideals it stood for, would soon turn to dust and disappear.

I planned on materializing a new, high-tech, hermetically sealed, bullet- and bombproof display case for the Constitution as well as the two other Charters of Freedom.

But first, I wanted to touch it. I *needed* to feel the document the way the founding fathers had felt it when they wrote down its vital words.

As soon as the tip of my finger touched the first sheet, I was blown away by a hurricane of emotions. So much so that I immediately (and involuntarily, I might add) dove down through the surface of time and went soaring back into history.

Hey, I've time-traveled before. I've even visited King Arthur's Court and hung out with Merlin (spoiler alert: he was an alien). But I've always been the one booking the flight and choosing the destination. I'd never before been swept up by a time-flux tsunami generated by raw, gut-wrenching emotion. I had no idea where or when I was headed—or why I was headed there—until I arrived.

I instantly recognized a lot of the men in powdered wigs, waistcoats, ruffled collars, and knee-high breeches milling around the room. George Washington, Benjamin Franklin, James Madison, and Alexander Hamilton were the most famous guys in the hall, but thirty-three other gentlemen were also present. All of them were eagerly awaiting their turn to pick up a feathered pen and affix their signatures to a freshly inked document.

Because I was in Philadelphia, in Independence Hall, standing with the thirty-nine founding fathers who had originally signed the United States Constitution.

Chapter 30

I WISHED I had brought along my kite.

Benjamin Franklin, his eyes twinkling, strolled over to greet me.

I have to admit: I'm a total Franklin fan-boy because, like me, he had interests all over the map. The guy—now best known for having his bald-headed picture on the hundred-dollar bill—was a famous author, printer, political theorist, postmaster, diplomat, statesman, scientist, and inventor (he came up with bifocals, the lightning rod, the odometer, and, of course, the Franklin stove). He also formed the first public lending library in America and the first fire department in Pennsylvania.

Then again, Benjamin Franklin was also the man who nominated the turkey to be America's national symbol (instead of the bald eagle), so not all of his ideas were absolutely brilliant. But, hey, the guy was always thinking.

"Ah, welcome to 1787, Daniel," he said, extending his

hand. "I always imagined time travel to be possible. As I've always said, one today is worth two tomorrows."

"That's why I'm here." I gestured toward the great men signing the document that every President of the United States takes an oath to preserve, protect, and defend. "This country's tomorrows aren't looking very bright, sir."

Franklin arched an eyebrow, wrinkling his high forehead. "Well, Daniel, our new Constitution only gives people the right to *pursue* happiness. You have to *catch* it all by yourself."

"It's the president. He's made some kind of deal with alien invaders."

"Alien invaders? Is it the French? The British, back for more?"

"No, sir. This alien is an extraterrestrial."

"Ah! A visitor from the heavens above?"

"I don't think this skeevy creep came from heaven, sir."

" 'Skeevy'?"

"Yeah. It's like a mix of sketchy and sleazy."

"Ah, yes. From the Italian *schifo*, for disgust."

"I guess. Anyway, this invader came from some other planet in some other solar system. Which one, I'm not sure. The List, my computer catalog of all the alien outlaws currently slinking around Earth, is very sketchy on this one's background."

Franklin pushed his bifocals up the bridge of his nose. "And this future President of the United States, he has allied himself with this evil ambassador?"

"Yes, sir. It's like you always said: 'He that lies down

with dogs, shall rise up with fleas.' The president is so totally flea-bitten he's telling the whole country to surrender, to become this alien's slaves!"

Franklin shook his head and tsked. "Slavery has always been a blight upon our country."

"But what should I do?"

"Simple. Educate the president. Offer him and all those who may agree with his decree a bit of advice: Those who would give up essential liberty to purchase a little temporary safety deserve neither liberty nor safety."

Now the great George Washington strode over to join us. "Remember, Daniel: Truth will ultimately prevail where there is pains taken to bring it to light."

"What do you suggest I do, General Washington?"

"Associate with people of good quality, for it is better to be alone than in bad company."

I nodded.

To save America, I needed to flee D.C. I needed to stick with people like Agent Judge and his FBI team. Joe, Willy, Emma, and Dana.

And, of course, Mel.

They didn't come much higher quality than her.

Chapter 31

AROUND MIDNIGHT I was at the wheel of the ATV, driving us back to Agent Judge's horse ranch. Agent Williams and Mel's dad were grabbing some much-needed shut-eye in the back of the truck. Mel was up front with me, trying her best to stay awake and keep me company as we rolled through the George Washington National Forest on the Appalachian border between Virginia and West Virginia.

Welcome to a typical day in my life: one minute you're chatting with George Washington, the next you're driving a high-tech Alien Tracking Vehicle through a forest named after him.

I had taken over steering-wheel duties from Agent Williams because, even though I'm not sixteen, I'm quite skilled at piloting all sorts of vehicles, many of which can travel faster than the speed of light. If necessary, I could also instantaneously generate an official, government-issued, hologram-stamped driver's license for whatever state an overzealous trooper might happen to pull us over in. Also, FYI, Alpar Nokians make excellent long-haul drivers because we need very little sleep. Especially after we chug a couple of Red Bulls.

"You okay, Daniel?" Mel asked through a mouth-stretching yawn.

"I'm fine. Get some sleep."

"No thanks. I'd rather stay up and keep you company."

"We still have another four or five hours till we reach Kentucky."

"Really?" Mel leaned over to check out the speedometer. "Even though you're doing, like, ninety in a fifty-five zone?"

"Don't worry. The highway patrol has other things to worry about tonight besides writing me a speeding ticket." It was true that the roads were completely empty—no cops, cars, even truckers.

"That's not what I'm worried about, Daniel." Mel's brow furrowed with concern. "I'm worried about *you*."

She reached over and placed a very warm, very comforting hand on my knee.

"It seems like this Number 2 is dead-set on destroying you," she continued. "For whatever twisted reason, he seems to be doing all...*this*...just to get at you."

"Not gonna happen," I said, even though I wasn't sure.

"Promise?" said Mel.

It was only one word, but I hadn't heard that much care and concern in a voice since the time I was two years old and my mother thought I had vanished from my crib.

(That was the day I accidentally discovered I could turn myself into inanimate objects and had become a stuffed monkey so I could chat with Schnozzy, my stuffed elephant.)

I raised my right hand to make a pledge: "Cross my heart and hope to have a water buffalo squat on my face."

"Huh?"

"It's something people used to say up on Alpar Nok. It's like a solemn vow."

"Well, I'm going to hold you to it."

"Hey, other aliens have tried to take me down before. They didn't have much luck. Neither will Number 2."

"Good," Mel said, settling back into her seat, resting her head against the pillow she'd made out of her jean jacket. "Because if that *thing* destroys you, well, that would totally destroy me."

Wow.

If I may be allowed to paraphrase a famous Oscar winner: She liked me. She really, really liked me.

I guess that's why, in the middle of the night, on a winding mountain road, I was loving this planet more than I had ever loved it.

Mel had her own amazing superpower: the uncanny ability to stir up emotions that had never been stirred before. For years, no living creature (except the ones I had cooked up in my imagination) had cared so much about me. Daniel X. The alien orphan kid with no last name, no *real* friends, no one to lose sleep worrying about him.

Until I met Mel.

Then again, I'd also have *no future* if Number 2 and his army of alien thugs had their way.

So, as much as I wished I could morph into a typical teenager and have my biggest burden be how to ask Mel to go horseback riding with me again, *saving the planet* was what I needed to focus on.

And with good reason.

Chapter 32

IT WAS 7 AM in New York City and 7 PM in Beijing when Abbadon struck next.

Amazingly, he was in both cities at the same time.

Astonishingly, he was also simultaneously in London (where it was noon) and Moscow (where it was 3 PM).

"I hope you are near a television, Daniel," Abbadon whispered to the winds whipping around him on his elevated posts in all four locations. "This is going to be *delicious*."

In New York Abbadon stood atop the Empire State Building; in Beijing he was out on the observation deck of a super-tall skyscraper called China World Trade Center III; in London he stood in an office window on the seventy-second floor of the unfinished London Bridge Tower; and in Moscow he chose the Naberezhnaya Building, which, at 881 feet, afforded him an excellent view of the chaos and destruction below.

"Witness my powers, Daniel! Fear me and bow down to me!"

In all four locations, buildings seemed to topple at his whim. Glass and steel and concrete slid down the sides of structures and crumbled to the ground as if the edifices were mammoth lizards losing several thick layers of skin.

In all four cities, Abbadon made the same bargain with the millions of panicked survivors filling the streets: "Serve me and live. Refuse me and die."

"What would you have us do?" pleaded the terrified leaders of the four metropolitan centers.

"Leave your families. Destroy your halls of justice. Burn all your books and abandon your churches. Take whatever you want from whomever you want to take it and join me in the underworld. And bring me the boy called Daniel!"

"Yes, Master!" a million voices cried out in reply.

"This is my planet now!" said Abbadon. "Only those who descend into the abyss to be my slaves shall escape the coming cataclysm."

"Yes, Master!"

Abbadon had never felt so close to total fulfillment.

All was now as it was always meant to be.

Chapter 33

EVERYBODY WAS WIDE awake when I parked the ATV in front of Xanthos's barn.

Our video monitors had just exploded with images of violent, catastrophic destruction.

Buildings toppled over. Fires raged. People rioted and looted and turned on one another.

If hanging out with Mel that day we went horseback riding was, according to my spiritual advisor, "experiencing humanity at its best," then what we were currently witnessing in high-definition surround sound was the flip side of that same coin: humanity at its absolute worst.

"He's hitting New York, London, Moscow, *and* Beijing!" exclaimed Agent Judge. "All at the same time."

Grainy images of mayhem from the four far-flung locations flickered across the screens. My eyes darted back and forth to verify what I was seeing. I could hear his voice cooing "Surrender to me!" in English and Russian and Chinese.

And then Number 2, cloaked in a black cape and seated in the saddles of four horses of different colors, rode triumphantly into the four live news feeds.

"This can't be happening," said Mel. "He can't really be in all four places at the same time. This has to be trick photography, or ... or he's totally defying the laws of physics."

"Yes," said her father. "This guy just *loves* breaking every law he can."

Number 2 also appeared to love quantum mechanics. Decades earlier, Earth scientists had discovered that it was, indeed, possible for subatomic particles, like electrons, to be in two different locations at the exact same instant. My guess was that Number 2 had figured out how to do the same thing on a macro scale.

And I had a hunch that maybe I could pull it off, too. I'd just have to concentrate on rearranging my own matter in four different directions.

Maybe. Theoretically.

And Mel *definitely* could not come with me this time.

Heck, I didn't even know if *I* could come with me. It'd be a brand-new, not to mention extraordinarily taxing, power.

"Don't worry," I said to Mel and Agent Judge. "I'll be back in a flash."

"Where are you going?" Mel asked. "Moscow? London?"

Her dad jumped in: "Beijing? New York?"

I just smiled at them both and said, "Yes."

Chapter 34

BEING IN FOUR places at the same time would be absolutely incredible if you could simultaneously watch a movie, catch a concert, eat a pizza, and, I don't know, scale a rock wall. It'd even be great if all you could do was go to the multiplex and watch four different movies at once.

But heading out to do battle with an archfiend in four different geographical hot spots?

Not so much.

Besides being a space-time aberration, it was a total multitasking nightmare. I was afraid my brain circuits would either fry or freeze up. Visually, it reminded me of that time I had turned myself into a housefly. But this time I wasn't just seeing kaleidoscopic images of the same thing repeatedly stacked up on top of itself.

Having achieved four-way-split teleportation, I was now seeing four very different real-time scenes simultaneously.

In London I could see Number 2, dressed in a tattered

black cloak like the grim reaper. He was carrying a crossbow and charging across the far horizon on the back of a white steed (I could tell the horse wasn't Xanthos because my spiritual advisor's eyeballs don't glow like red LEDs).

Number 2 must've just looted the fallen ruins of the Tower of London, because on his hooded head I could see the glistening diamonds, pearls, sapphires, emeralds, and rubies he had obviously stolen from the Tower's Crown Jewels collection.

"I have crowned myself your conqueror!" he cried out to the masses scurrying through London's narrow lanes. "Serve me and live. Refuse me and die!"

Across the ocean, on the island of Manhattan, I couldn't catch up with Number 2 as he rode a fiery red horse up Broadway and, swinging a sword over his head, helped his scorpion-tailed henchbeasts cattle-prod a herd of terror-stricken New Yorkers up the street to the nearest subway entrances.

"You are the spoils of war!" he shouted. "Serve me!"

He was also on horseback in China, where the galloping stallion was black. For some bizarre-o reason, in Beijing Number 2 carried a pair of market scales instead of a weapon and cried out, "Slaves will find food in their bellies; resistors will starve!" Hungry multitudes raced after Number 2's minions and followed them down into the Beijing subway stations.

Moscow was even worse. For just an instant, I saw Number 2 as he trotted through what was left of Red

Square. The spiral onion-dome towers of St. Basil's Cathedral lay atop a heap of rubble like multicolored swirl cones somebody had dropped on a litter-strewn boardwalk.

In Moscow I could also smell Number 2 something fierce.

The black-caped creep carried the scent of a rotting side of beef jammed into a refrigerator that had stopped working weeks ago.

He smelled like death.

To complete the death theme, the pale horse he rode through the Russian wreckage was the color of a corpse— a sort of sickly yellowish green with pus-colored blotches all over its hindquarters.

"I am death to those who do not heed my call!"

The me in Moscow didn't chase after the extremely grim reaper as his horse leaped over the shattered red star that used to top the turret of the Vodovzvodnaya Tower.

Because there was another problem within spitting distance.

A *gopnik*.

A street gang of tough young males with razor-cut hair and glazed "I don't care" eyes. They were decked out in jogging suits and had just circled a babushka, a little old lady with few good teeth and a headscarf tied under her chin.

I sensed what was about to happen.

This Moscow street gang was going to have some end-of-the-world fun by mugging, and maybe murdering, somebody's grandmother!

Chapter 35

I IMMEDIATELY SHUT down the whole quantum-leap experiment and pulled myself together on the mean streets of Moscow.

I couldn't let these hooligans hurt the defenseless old woman, not if I ever wanted to face myself in the mirror again. For now, I needed to concentrate all my powers in this one location: Red Square.

I also needed my friends.

"What's up?" said Joe, when he, Willy, Emma, and Dana materialized.

"We need to teach these young Muscovites a thing or two about respecting their elders," I said as the five of us surrounded the two dozen bad dudes circling the babushka.

"Might be time to call in the heavy artillery," suggested Willy.

"Yeah," agreed Dana. "Make these tough guys cry Mayday."

An excellent suggestion, I thought, since Mayday is the

international distress signal, and May Day is also very close to Victory Day in Russia, a holiday when the old Soviet empire used to parade rocket launchers and tanks and goose-stepping troops through this very same square. I skipped the soldiers and concentrated on the big guns.

Twenty-four tanks and twenty-four nuclear-tipped rocket launchers rumbled into the square, one of each aimed directly at each of the twenty-four thugs threatening the defenseless granny. Clanking tank treads and rumbling truck tires crunching across chunks of concrete definitely got the bad boys' attention. All twenty-four of them twirled around to face us and our newly arrived backup.

"Give it up, guys," I called out. "You're seriously outgunned. Let her go."

"Who are you?" jeered their leader. "Are you with the horseman?"

"No," said Dana, swaggering forward. "We're the good guys."

Now the leader violently grabbed the babushka and wrapped his arm around her throat. "Then call off your tanks!" he snarled. "Pull back your missiles. Or I will kill this old woman! I will kill her now!"

"You don't want to do that, my friend," said Willy, stealthily moving forward, ready to pounce the second I gave him the go signal.

"*Da!* I do!" The gang leader snarled, tightening his vise-like grip on the babushka's throat. "This old woman has lived long enough." He raised a jagged vodka bottle he held clutched in his right fist. "There is no room for old ones such as her down below. Our new Lord and Master does not need weaklings."

"Drop the bottle, buddy," said Willy, both hands up and ready to rock.

The gang leader just laughed. "Or what, little boy? You will take it from me?"

Dana moved forward boldly. "No. I will."

"Pah! You are a girl!"

"Good eye, Boris Badenov. Now play nice and hand over your bottle. If you do, I'll give you a binky to suck on instead."

Dana leaped forward just as I was just about to turn the Russian's nasty-looking jagged bottle into a floppy, harmless fish.

But the gang leader slashed at Dana's face with the thing an instant before I made the switch.

Her hands flew up to the bleeding wound.

Thinking fast—finally—I turned the gang of hoodlums, all of whom were reaching for weapons, into Red Square's newest tableau of frozen bronze statues, something I should've done six nanoseconds sooner, but my reflexes were still foggy from the four-location stunt I had just pulled off (not to mention my massive military buildup in Red Square).

"Take care of the babushka," I called to Emma, who raced over to comfort the elderly woman while the rest of us ran to help Dana.

But Granny didn't want comforting. "Where two are fighting, third should not interfere!" she hissed at Emma before scuttling off through the logjam of tanks and rocket launchers to join the crowd of Muscovites mauling one another at the entrance to a nearby subway station.

Emma dashed back to see how Dana was doing. Blood was dribbling out of the gash on her cheek.

I felt sick. I'd sworn I'd never let my friends get hurt again—especially Dana.

This was a failure I wasn't prepared to accept.

Chapter 36

"WHAT'S THE MATTER, Daniel?" Dana said, gritting her teeth to smile through the pain.

"I'm *so*, so sorry, Dana! I-I don't know what happened. My response time is lousy right now...my brain must be out to lunch...."

"Chya," Dana said, chuffing out a nose laugh. "Whatever, Dr. Danny. Can you just focus on fixing up my face?"

"You got it."

I was able to stanch the blood without lifting a finger.

"She still has a scar," whispered Emma.

I focused on it, tried to erase it from her face, to imagine it away.

But I couldn't.

It was still there.

"Um, are you okay, Daniel?" asked Emma. "Maybe you shouldn't have tried that being-in-four-places-at-the-same-time trick."

"Or whipped up all the heavy artillery," added Willy.

"Yeah," said Joe. "Maybe you left a few of your super-powers back in London or Beijing."

"Just fix Dana, will you?" blurted Willy.

"I'm trying," I said, sounding way more defensive than I ever want to sound again.

"You can do it, Danny," said Joe. "Since Dana's a product of your imagination, just imagine her looking the way she's supposed to."

"Is it bad?" Dana asked, trying to check out her reflection in the lenses of Joe's glasses.

"Nah," said Willy. "It's just a tiny little nick. But, well, I always think of you as being, you know, totally perfect."

When Willy said that, Dana fluttered her eyelashes. She might've even blushed. "You do?"

"Well, yeah," Willy said very shyly, slightly embarrassed. All of a sudden, I got the funny feeling that some of my more personal opinions about my dream girl had seeped out of my mind and found their way over to my imagined *guy* friend, because Willy sure sounded like he had a mad crush on Dana, too.

"Well, that's sweet, Willy," Dana said, smirking. "But I have news for you: it's just a little scar. No big deal. I'm still perfect for you, Willy!"

For you. I gulped even though I knew Dana was trying to make me feel jealous about her and Willy the way I had made her feel jealous about Mel and me. Yep, even for Alien Hunters, being a teenager is one big, complicated, boy-girl, he said/she said mess.

"Okay, so if Danny boy's not working any miracles

here, then let's go grab some cheese blintzes and shish kebab–flavored potato chips," urged Joe. "Moscow's famous for 'em — and I'm so hungry, I could eat a horse. Even that gnarly green nag Number 2 was riding."

That's when it finally struck me: Xanthos had told me to be on the lookout for strangely colored equestrian creatures....

Know this: a red horse shall be a sign, he had advised, adding that the red horse would be *a sign of all that is written, of all that must be.*

The *red* horse had been in New York City, not Moscow.

I had pulled myself together in the wrong location!

Chapter 37

I FLEW SOLO to New York City.

Actually, I teleported there, a skill my dad had taught me a while back. But to pull it off, I need to fully grok the topography of where I want to go and do some serious GPS mental gymnastics. As you might guess, such intense grokation requires a ton of focus, so, typically, I don't bring along any excess cargo, like my four best friends.

I sort of wished I had at least *tried* to bring Joe, Willy, Emma, and Dana. For a couple of reasons.

Reason one: I felt horrible about abandoning Dana before I completely healed her. Joe and Willy were right: Dana is a hundred-percent pure product of *my* imagination. I should have been able to erase any trace of the wound simply by imagining Dana the way I always imagine her. But, for whatever reason, it wasn't working.

This logic problem made me wonder: Did I subconsciously want to leave Dana slightly "flawed" as I kept falling deeper and deeper for Mel? I might need to check in with Dr. Phil or Xanthos on that one.

Reason two for wishing I had brought the gang: I sure could've used some backup going up against Number 2. If the guy could turn the Empire State Building into a trash heap even King Kong wouldn't recognize, what could he do to me?

I popped into New York a full ten city blocks away from Number 2, but he was extremely easy to spot because he was the only speck of color in an otherwise bleak landscape. He sat astride his bright red horse in a crater-strewn plane of gray dust and destruction. Using my telephoto vision, I zoomed in on the black-hooded beast as he and his scarlet stallion pranced around the ruins of Grand Central Terminal, the city's biggest commuter train station. A mob of New Yorkers was pushing and shoving its way down mangled staircases to the subterranean train tracks.

And New Yorkers really know how to push and shove.

"Get outta my way!" I heard somebody shout.

"Are you talking to me?" an angry man shouted back. "Are *you* talking to *me*?"

Meanwhile, Number 2 calmly circled the madness on horseback, looking like an NYPD mounted cop nonchalantly patrolling the city's annual Thanksgiving Day Parade. When a fistfight broke out between a bunch of guys in Yankees caps and another group in Mets hats, he just reared up on his crimson steed and laughed.

My disgust for this alien invader was about to overwhelm me.

How dare he destroy this planet and enslave all of its people?

Suddenly I felt a buzzing in my chest.

I figured my anger was raging so intensely it was ratcheting up my blood pressure.

Sorry, Xanthos, I thought. I was about to give sway to the negative way—big-time. I was going to obliterate Number 2 before he got the chance to demolish any more of the world I had vowed to protect.

The buzzing in my chest intensified.

I touched my jacket and realized I had set my cell phone on vibrate.

I pulled the quivering thing out of its pocket. Mel's image was glowing on the call screen.

"Daniel? Where are you?"

"New York."

I could hear Xanthos whinnying in the background, so she must have been calling me from inside the horse barn.

Then I could hear his voice in my head.

Choose wisely, my yute. Do not gain the world and lose your soul.

You said the red horse would be a sign! I telepathically thought back at him. *A sign of what?*

What is written in the book.

What book?

All of them.

"Daniel?" Mel spoke again. "I'm not so sure about this

multiple-personality thing. It'd be great having four of you to hang out with, but I want the *one* guy I've ever really, really liked to come home. *Now*, please!"

Home? I thought. *I have no home.* Number 1 had made certain of that, years ago, when he wiped out my entire family. And now Number 2 was laying waste to everything on the surface of what had become my adopted home. Earth.

"I'm sorry, Mel, but I feel like there's a bomb inside my chest that's going to explode if I don't take out this creep right here, right now."

"Wait a second, Daniel...." I heard Mel cry as I flung my phone to the ground.

Do not give sway to the negative...

"Shut up, you stupid horse!" I yelled. Call ended.

Furious, I bounded up into the air and soared ten blocks above the horde of rowdy New Yorkers fighting for their chance to hop on an express train down to Number 2's slave pens.

When I landed, Number 2 was standing right in front of me, but his flaming-red stallion was nowhere to be seen.

We were face-to-face in the pile of marble and tile that used to be Grand Central's magnificent main concourse. I could feel Number 2's foul, death-stench breath chilling my whole body.

"Hello, Daniel," he said with a sneer. "I see that I have finally earned your *undivided* attention."

"Whatever!" I sneered back. "Fight me. Right here. Right now."

My challenge seemed to amuse the colossal freak. "Don't be absurd, Daniel. This isn't as it should be."

"I said *fight me*. Come on." I poked out my chin to give him an easy target. "Give me your best shot."

I was so blinded by my rampaging rage that I hadn't worked out exactly *how* I was going to defeat this demon. I figured once we were fighting, inspiration would hit me. I'd improvise a winning strategy *after* Number 2 showed me exactly what I was up against.

"Fight me!" I hollered again.

Number 2 smiled. Then something hit me—*BAM!*—right on the chin.

And it sure wasn't inspiration.

In a blindingly fast, hypersonic instant, Number 2 socked me with a punch so powerful it knocked me straight into tomorrow.

Literally!

PART TWO

MARCHING TOWARD ARMAGEDDON

Chapter 38

I LANDED ON my butt in front of what used to be the Chrysler Building, just up Forty-second Street from Grand Central Terminal.

I knew it was the Chrysler Building because I recognized the bashed-in steel beaks of the eagle-head gargoyles that used to stare out at the city from the ledges of the sixty-first floor. The eagles were replicas of Chrysler hood ornaments from 1929. Talk about a time warp: I was sitting in tomorrow, staring at a relic of yesterday.

The streets, which before had been so crowded with throngs of jostling New Yorkers elbowing and stiff-arming one another as they ran down the subway stairs, were now totally deserted. So I had a sneaking suspicion that I wasn't in exactly the same space-time continuum I'd occupied a second earlier.

After gaining my bearings I noticed that I wasn't completely alone. A man was scavenging his way across the scrap heap of the Chrysler Building, digging through the debris, looking for anything edible he could find. He danced a little jig when he rolled over a boulder and uncovered what had once been the lobby's snack shop.

While he helped himself to a whole carton of plastic-wrapped Oreos packets, I climbed over the rocky remains of the collapsed art deco masterpiece to talk to him.

"Where is everybody?"

My voice startled the guy. He whipped his head around while nibbling his way around the black edges of the cookie like a rat working its way around a wheel of cheese. I couldn't help making the rat comparison, since a squealing pack of wiry-tailed rodents scurried around his ankles, helping themselves to the treasure trove of crushed candy bars, cookies, and chips he had just uncovered.

The man didn't answer. He just kept staring at me with a terrified look in his eyes.

So I asked again. Louder this time. *"Where did everybody go, sir?"*

"Who are you, kid? Where'd you come from?"

"I'm Daniel. And let's just skip the where. It's complicated. Who are you?"

"Bob," the man replied. He had a week's worth of stubble on his cheeks, not to mention a week's worth of grime on his clothes. He wore a tattered raincoat, a soiled shirt, baggy pants belted by a frayed rope, and bundles of plastic bags on his feet for shoes.

"Did you see that mob of people at Grand Central?" I asked.

"Yesterday."

"Where did they all go?"

Bob pointed a shaky finger toward the scrap heap that had been the railroad terminal. "Below. Down with the horseman. Yesterday was the end of the world, unless you were sleeping inside a Dumpster."

That's when I fully understood what had happened. Somehow, a single blow from Number 2 had sent me spiraling *forward* through time, something I had never done before and, frankly, wasn't really interested in doing again anytime soon.

"He rode a red horse!" Bob shouted. "The second seal has been broken. He was the second horseman of the Apocalypse."

Maybe, I thought.

I had seen all four steeds, but I hadn't yet put two and two together to figure out that the alien invader was trying to terrify the world by aping the Four Horsemen of the Apocalypse, who, the Book of Revelation predicted, would ride a white horse, a red horse, a black horse, and a pale (or puke-green) horse.

"'Then another horse came out, a fiery red one,'" Bob ranted, recalling the ancient text. "'Its rider was given power to take peace from the Earth and to make men slay each other. To him was given a large sword!'"

My turn to nod. I had seen Number 2's sword, too.

And if this really was tomorrow, I had lost more than a day.

I had also lost Number 2. The second-most-lethal alien outlaw on Terra Firma (or what was left of it) had at least a twenty-four-hour jump on me.

I needed to talk with Xanthos. After all, it was my spiritual advisor who had advised me to be on the lookout for a red horse. Maybe he could drop me a few more hints. Like how to end Number 2's world by giving him his own personal Armageddon.

"Nice meeting you, Bob," I said. "Maybe I'll see you again."

"When? There will be no more tomorrows!"

"Well, then maybe I'll see you *yesterday*, because that's where I'm going."

Hey, I may not know how to pull a fast-forward without someone sucker-punching me in the chin, but I'm an old hand at time-traveling *backward*!

Chapter 39

IN AN INSTANT, I was back in Kentucky—and back in time.

In fact, Mel had her cell phone out.

"Wow," she said. "I was just about to call you."

Apparently I had picked up a few extra minutes and landed in yesterday *before* Mel had gone into the horse barn to make her phone call to me in New York. If I had yet to save the world from the wrath of Number 2, at least I was saving Mel some minutes on her dad's monthly phone bill.

Mel threw her arms around my neck and hugged me like she never wanted to let me go—*or* to let me go anywhere ever again. To be honest, the idea of mucking horse stalls with Mel for the rest of my life sounded like the most totally awesome thing I have ever imagined and, as you know, I can imagine some amazingly incredible stuff.

I savored the moment. For a full five seconds.

"So, how about you don't do that again," Mel said as we

came out of our embrace. "*One* Daniel is hard enough to keep up with."

"Are you okay?" I asked.

"You mean other than being worried sick about a certain Alien Hunter?"

"Yeah."

"I'm fine. Dad says we're totally safe here. His whole squad is camped out in the house, in the barn, out in the fields. And they're decked out with all kinds of ray guns and junk they've confiscated from extraterrestrial outlaws."

I had a hunch I had already seen most of the alien weaponry they were armed with at some point in time, when it had been aimed at *me*.

"I need to check in with Xanthos," I told Mel.

"What do you want us to do?" asked Joe.

Yes, my "squad" was in Kentucky, too. Joe was chowing down on a bucket of Extra Crispy KFC, a box of Colonel's Crispy Strips, and a tub of Popcorn Chicken. Emma was over in the paddock, petting a pony. Willy and Dana were in the barnyard, standing beside Joe.

Holding hands.

"What's next, Daniel?" Dana asked, trying to seem nonchalant.

I knew Dana wasn't just asking about what was going to happen next in our battle against Number 2. She was wondering what came next for *us*.

Before I could answer, she said, "Think about it. In the meantime, Willy and I are going for a walk."

"We are?" Willy looked pleasantly surprised.

Dana cuddled up closer to him. "You want to see what's behind that horse barn, don't you?"

Willy's face went beet red. "I guess. I mean, if it's okay with you, Daniel."

"Sure," I said. "We have time. I need to check in with Xanthos, work up a plan."

"A plan might be good," Dana said, giving me a look. Then she leaned up to whisper something in Willy's ear.

His face went from beet red to I-just-ate-a-pound-of-jalapeño-poppers red.

"Are you okay?" Mel asked as I watched Dana and Willy, strolling hand in hand, disappear behind the barn.

"Yeah," I said. "I'm fine."

"You sure? You don't mind Dana and Willy's nonstop PDA activity?"

"That? Nah. I'm cool. I couldn't care less about them. Hey, I have a world to save, remember?"

Mel faked a smile and acted like she believed me.

Heck, I didn't believe me, either.

Chapter 40

XANTHOS WAS LYING down in his stall, his head fully erect, his eyes locked on mine.

I was sitting yoga-style with my legs crossed in a corner.

Our minds were totally linked.

Tell me about Number 2, I said telepathically.

What is it you would know, Daniel?

Anything and everything.

Xanthos snorted a horse-sized sigh through both of his nostrils. *What have you learned, my brudda? What have you seen?*

Um, in case you don't watch TV, Number 2 is out there destroying the entire planet, and from what I've seen so far, I don't think he's giving free passes to horses. So if you don't mind, can we do this a little more expeditiously?

Do you mean faster?

Yes! For starters, how about you don't answer every question I ask with another question!

Do you think that would help your cause?

Yes! Who is Number 2?

He is one who calls himself Abbadon. The Destroyer. He is known in some sacred texts to be the king of tormenting locusts and the angel of the bottomless pit.

Okay, I've seen the locusts. But trust me, this Abbadon is no angel.

You speak true. You see, Daniel, you, your father, your mother, and even your friends outside, you came to this planet to protect it. Abbadon, on the other hand, came here to destroy it.

Wait a second—did my dad and Abbadon come to this planet at the same time? Is this some sort of yin-yang cosmic balancing act? Is the universe somehow trying to keep things even-steven by tossing in one creator and one destroyer?

Xanthos shook his head. *No, my yute. Abbadon has been around for a long, long year—stirring up trouble, fomenting chaos, turning humans against one another.*

I remembered the people mauling one another in New York City. The street gang in Moscow. The Chinese stampeding to board the subway trains. All those humans were seriously lacking in kindness, compassion, and goodwill. In other words, Abbadon had successfully stripped them of anything resembling humanity.

I stood up, dusted straw off my jeans.

Okay—what do we do next? How do we destroy The Destroyer?

Xanthos closed his eyes. This time when he sighed, I felt his sadness. *Why do you wish to do as the evil one has done? Don't bury your thoughts under his vision. Flee from hate, mischief, and—*

Wait a second. So far, this Abbadon has totally wiped out New York, Washington, London, Moscow, Beijing, and just about everywhere in between! And you want me to flee?

No, Daniel. I want you to be true to who you are: Create where others destroy. Build up what they tear down.

Fine. I'll work on that, right after I tear down this Abbadon.

Very well. It is your river to cross, brudda.

Suddenly I had a thought. *Is this why The List is so sketchy on Number 2? Did Abbadon destroy all the intel we'd gathered on him during his centuries of troublemaking here on Earth?*

Perhaps.

Thanks. That's really, really helpful. I was being sarcastic. Some advisor you turned out to be.

For your spirit, Daniel. Your soul. We each have our role and must play it as written.

I took a deep breath. Counted to ten, then to twenty. I knew I was letting my anger get the best of me, and when I'm about to lose my temper I can't create anything, not even those cheap, flavorless globules that cost a quarter in gumball machines.

Truth is, I was mad at the situation, not at Xanthos.

Okay. As my spiritual advisor, what would you suggest I do next?

Xanthos rose up on his sturdy legs. When he whinnied merrily, I knew we were still "bredren"—brothers in unity.

Perhaps dinner with your friends, yah, mon?

What? Number 2 or Abbadon or whatever he calls himself is still out there, still knocking down skyscrapers, and you want me to sit back, relax, and enjoy the flight?

Abbadon has gone underground.

You're sure?

Do not worry, Daniel. You will face him again. When the time comes.

And when's that?

Ah, this I do not know. However, the next time you will have no need to hunt Abbadon down. When all is in readiness, he will come for you!

Chapter 41

I DID AS Xanthos advised: I sat down to dinner that night with Mel, Agent Judge, Joe, Emma, Willy, and Dana.

And by "Willy and Dana" I mean *Willy-n-Dana*, like you'd see carved into the bark of a tree or graffitied on a small-town water tower.

They were sitting side by side, their chairs pushed a little closer together than all the others around the knotty-pine farmhouse table. From the grin on Dana's face and the giddy bewilderment on Willy's, I think they might have been playing footsie under the table, too.

As if that weren't bad enough, I once again noticed the slender white line running from Dana's eye to her chin. No matter how hard I tried, I couldn't make that scar disappear!

Mel reached over to touch my hand. I guess she'd been watching me watching them.

"Is everything okay, Daniel?"

"Hmm?"

"You look like you're here but your mind is off some-where else."

"Yeah, buddy," said Joe. "You look a little out to lunch, which is too bad, because this *dinner* is awesome. What do you call this soup, Agent Judge?"

"That's Kentucky Burgoo," replied Mel's dad.

"It's so thick, I could stand my spoon up in it—if I wasn't busy using my spoon to eat it. What's in it?"

"Mixed meat. Beef, lamb, pork, chicken. Tomatoes and celery and a couple of potatoes. Spices and Worcestershire sauce."

"Don't worry," Mel said to Emma. "I made yours and mine with just the vegetables, and none of the chicken or beef stock."

"I appreciate it," said Emma. "As do the cows, the lambs, the pigs, and the chickens."

We all had a chuckle over that.

"Well, don't blame me, Emma," said Agent Judge. "It's my late wife's recipe." When he said that, his eyes looked a little sad.

"So, Daniel," asked Willy, "what did your horse say we should do next?"

I gestured toward the dinner table, laden with plates and serving dishes. "This."

"You're kidding," said Dana. "He told you to eat Ken-tucky Burgoo?"

"Basically."

"Best spiritual advisor ever," proclaimed Joe. "Did he also suggest the Derby pie for dessert? Because it looks *amazing*. Like a chocolate-walnut candy bar wrapped inside piecrust!"

"He also told me that when the time comes, Abbadon will bring the fight to me."

"Abba-dabba who?" said Mel.

"Abbadon. That's the name Number 2's given himself, so I did a quick Google search on it." I tapped my head, indicating my built-in Wi-Fi access. "In the Book of Revelation, at the very end of the Bible, Abbadon is described as the king of the bottomless pit and the leader of a legion of beasts with locust wings and scorpion tails."

Dana put down her spoon. "Like those things that attacked us on the bridge back in D.C.?"

"And probably would've torn us all to pieces," said Emma, "if Mel hadn't blasted them with those ultrasonic waves."

Mel shrugged. "I improvised. You guys would've done the same thing."

Dana was looking uncomfortable, so I figured it was time to change the subject. "Agent Judge? I'm a little worried about security. If Abbadon is going to bring the fight to me, he and his troops could come here."

"Rest easy. My men have set up an impenetrable perimeter around the entire property."

He gestured toward the matrix of high-tech security screens built into the dining room wall. We could see FBI agents armed with heavy alien weaponry patrolling the white fence line of the horse ranch.

The hulking navy cook came in from the kitchen, sporting a hand blaster strapped on under the strings of his stain-splotched apron. "You guys still have room for dessert, right?" said the chef.

"You bet," said Joe.

"Always," added Mel.

"Good," said the cook. "Because an army marches on its stomach."

"And retreats on its butt," said Joe.

We had another laugh and, somehow, everybody at the table, including the cook, who sat down to join us, managed to find just enough room for a slice or two of Derby pie.

Things stayed pretty quiet until Joe scraped the pie plate clean with his fork and the rest of us leaned back in our chairs to digest the feast.

"Was the pie your wife's recipe, too?" asked Emma.

"Yes," said Agent Judge softly. "It was."

"I'm sorry for your loss," Emma said to both Agent Judge and Mel.

"Thanks, Emma," said Mel.

"Did she pass away recently?"

Mel shook her head. "No. A long time ago."

Agent Judge didn't say anything right away. Instead, he turned to me. "I guess that's something else you and Mel have in common."

"Sir?"

"You both lost your mothers at an early age."

I nodded, but I wasn't ready for what he said next.

"And they were both murdered by the same beast."

"Number 1?"

Mel nodded.

"When he was finished at your house," she said, "he came to ours."

Chapter 42

TO MAKE ABSOLUTELY certain Agent Judge and Mel didn't suffer any more losses because of me and my presence under their roof, I took the gang on an after-dinner stroll around the ranch.

"I love taking a long walk after dinner," Emma said, drinking in the cool night air. "The sky is so crisp and clear. Look at all those stars."

"Hey, Daniel, I think I can see your house from here," Joe said, pointing at a tiny twinkling dot on the eastern horizon.

"It's *so* romantic," Dana said, squeezing Willy's hand.

Yes, the two of them were *still* holding hands.

"Not to be a downer, guys," I said, "but we have work to do. I want to make one hundred percent certain security is airtight."

We came upon two FBI agents on sentry duty.

"Evening, folks," said one.

"State your business," said the other.

"I'm Daniel. These are my friends. We're double-checking Agent Judge's security setup."

"We're locked and loaded," said the brusque one, brandishing an RJ-57 tritium-charged bazooka powerful enough to drill all the presidents on Mount Rushmore new nostrils. "No one, alien or human, gets in or out without passing a checkpoint."

"We have teams set up every hundred meters along the fence line," said the other one, who was toting a high-intensity microwave pistol some alien outlaw must've dropped in a firefight with the IOU. "But I have to admit, our air defenses are a little weak. I wish we had more than a standard radar package and the HAWK surface-to-air missile system."

"I wish we had a big glass dome," said his gruff partner. "Like in *The Simpsons Movie*."

I grinned. I *loved* that movie—and I thought the bazooka-toting FBI guy's idea was brilliant! So while he hummed a few bars of "Spider Pig," I closed my eyes and started thinking about an upside-down teacup four miles wide and about a mile deep. A teacup made out of an impenetrable plastic polymer, thirty feet thick.

When I opened my eyes, the stars in the sky were a little fuzzier, a little blurred around the edges. When I checked the top of the dome, the constellations on the other side looked kind of warped, as if the stars were staring at themselves in a fun-house mirror.

"Willy?"

"Yeah?"

"You want to do the honors?"

"Absolutely." He turned to the sentry with the micro-wave ray gun. "Can I borrow your pistol, sir?"

"Huh?"

"I need to test your newly enhanced air defenses."

The FBI agent, not entirely sure what Willy was talking about, reluctantly handed over his weapon.

"Thanks." Willy aimed the pistol up over his head and squeezed the trigger.

A microsecond later, an undulating aurora of brilliantly colored light radiated out from the impact point and, for an instant, illuminated the curve of the dome.

"Outstanding," said the man with the bazooka. "Just like *The Simpsons Movie*."

"Yeah," I said. "Oh, and one more thing: you should probably tell your guards not to venture fifty feet forward from the fence line."

"How come?"

"Joe?"

Joe bent down, picked up a hefty rock the size of a soft-ball, and chucked it toward the horizon.

When the stone hit the interior lining of the dome, it exploded into a puff of dust. We could all hear a shower of gritty sand particles sprinkling to the ground.

Both FBI guys nodded.

"Gotcha," said the one.

"Good to know," said the other.

"Um, Daniel?" said Joe. "Quick question."

"Fire away."

"You'll take down the dome for food deliveries, right?"

"Don't worry," I said, "I've already stocked the pantry. If we run out of Doritos or Ring Dings, I'll stock it again."

Joe let out a huge sigh of relief. "Awesome."

Chapter 43

"IF ABBADON WAS thinking about bringing the fight to us tonight," Willy said as we headed back to the farmhouse, "I'm afraid he'll have to change his plans!"

"Absolutely," said Emma.

"What kind of name is that, anyway?" asked Dana. "'Abbadon.' It sounds like he's some kind of Swedish pop group. Maybe he's a fan. Probably knows all the words to 'Mamma Mia.'"

"That song has words?" said Joe. "I mean other than 'mamma' and 'mia'?"

"Hey, look," Willy said, bending down to examine a shadowy clump. "A whole pile of horseshoes."

"Let's play!" said Emma. "Come on! We've all been so keyed up these last couple of days. We need to blow off a little steam."

"I agree," I said. "We deserve a little R and R."

"Okay, see that weather vane on top of the horse barn?"

said Willy, pointing to the moonlit silhouette a half mile away. "The pole holding it up is our target."

"Me and Willy against you three!" Dana said, scooting over to latch on to Willy's arm.

"No way," said Willy.

"What?" said Dana. She sounded kind of like an eighth grader who'd just heard from her girlfriend that her boyfriend had talked to some guy who said that this other guy heard some guy in the locker room say Willy didn't like Dana anymore.

"Daniel's too good," Willy explained. "It should be all *four* of us against him."

"Yeah," Joe and Emma agreed as they sidled up alongside Willy and Dana.

"Fine," I said with a grin. "Bring it on."

"Alpar Nokian rules?" asked Willy.

"Definitely."

"Okay," said Emma, "that means zero points for leaners."

"And zero points for being the closest to the pole," added Joe.

"And, of course," said Dana, "you have to turn your back to the target and toss the horseshoe over your shoulder."

"While hopping up and down on your nondominant foot," added Emma.

We all nodded. On Alpar Nok, instead of horseshoes, the contestants hurled giant metal booties worn by domesticated elephants across great distances at flaming torches planted in the turf. If you knocked out the fire by flinging your bootie straight through the flame, you earned ten points. If you snuffed it out by landing your bootie upside down on top of the flame, you got a Douser, worth fifty points (not to mention first dibs on the deviled eggs).

"We go first!" said Joe.

"Fire away," I said.

I heard the familiar whir and whistle of wobbly steel flying through the air. It was soon followed by the clank of a spinning horseshoe grabbing hold of a metal rod 30 feet up and 2,640 feet away.

And then, in very rapid succession, I heard that clank three more times.

"Four ringers!" shouted Dana. "How are you going to beat that, Daniel?"

"I'm not sure," I said, turning my back to the barn, hopping up on my left foot. "Maybe like this?"

I flicked my horseshoe backward, right over the top of my head.

Then I spun around to watch it spiral and soar across the sky until it wrapped itself around the torso of the flying-horse ornament poised on top of the weather vane. The arch of metal hit the horse at extremely high velocity, and it ripped the whole weather vane rig right off the roof, tearing out its anchor bolts and sending it flying. Naturally, this caused all four of my friends' horseshoes to slide off the support post and clink, one by one, down to the ground below.

"Yes!" I cheered, triumphantly raising my arms to celebrate my spectacular victory.

I was staring straight up at the top of the dome.

Surprisingly, the Milky Way didn't look smudged or milky.

In fact, all the stars were once again crisp, clear, and sparkling.

It was almost as if, while I was busy ripping the weather vane off the barn, someone had ripped a hole in my impenetrable security shield!

Chapter 44

ABBADON STOOD, SURROUNDED by his minions, in a charred meadow a hundred yards east of the white stockade fence surrounding the FBI agent's horse farm.

"Foolish boy," he whispered to the wind. "Did you not see what I did to New York, London, Beijing, Moscow, and the rest? Did you really think your idiotic dome would remain impenetrable? To me?"

He shook his head.

He wondered if this Daniel would ever prove himself the worthy adversary he had been promised.

"Whatever you create, child, I can just as easily destroy!"

He fluttered open his massive set of wings.

"Fly!" he shouted to the pack of warriors he had brought with him to Kentucky. On his command, the aliens clustered in the flattened field once again morphed into inky black bats. Squealing, the swarm took flight and blotted out the starlit sky. They zoomed to the west and shot through the gaping hole Abbadon had so easily punched in Daniel's protective shield.

Abbadon watched as his minions, using their innate radar systems, swooped under and around the latticework of unseen laser-beam triggers crisscrossing the airspace around the Judges' farm. Once clear of the alarm grid, the bats skimmed across the open fields, flying inches above the ground, remaining undetected by the humans' mechanical and, therefore, less-effective radar systems. The flock split in two. One squad rocketed toward the main house while the other zoomed off to the barn.

To deal with that one, thought Abbadon. *The interloper.*

When the twin sorties reached their targets, the bats zoomed straight up the sides of the buildings. The house squad dive-bombed down the chimneys. The barn squadron simply slipped through the crack between the sliding front doors.

"We're in," both leaders reported back.

"Excellent," said Abbadon. "Complete your missions."

"Yes, Master," the leaders grunted.

"And remember, do not hurt the girl. Ferry her down below."

"What about Xanthos?" asked the leader in the barn.

"Eliminate him," Abbadon replied easily. "He has been giving Daniel an unfair advantage."

Chapter 45

I CAN OUTRUN hummingbirds and Japanese bullet trains. My personal best speed used to be 438 mph. Nobody was clocking me on this particular night, but I think I topped that as I shot across the half mile of open field to the farmhouse. My sonic boom shattered a couple of windows in Agent Judge's antique pickup truck.

I had seen a swarm of scuzzy bats plunge down the chimney pipes and knew, instantly, what was going on: Number 2 was sending in his creeps from the cave. They'd morph out of their flying mammal mode and switch back into their hideous alien selves the instant they were inside.

But why? What did they want in the house?

I was out in the yard. *My* face was the one on the WANTED poster. I was the Alien Hunter with an unbelievably hefty bounty on his head.

So why did the bats storm into Agent Judge's house?

Unfortunately, Agent Judge soon gave me the answer.

I burst in through the front door and saw him in the

parlor, swinging a laser-sighted blaster right, left, up, down—searching for a target.

"They grabbed her!"

"What?"

"The aliens took Mel!"

Chapter 46

"THEY'RE IN THE barn!" Willy shouted as soon as we'd bolted outside. Someone had pushed the doors wide open.

"I heard whinnies and screams," reported Emma. "I think they're torturing the horses!"

"Cover us!" I called to Agent Judge, who was joined by maybe a dozen other FBI agents, all of them hauling heavy E.T. hardware. They took up firing positions behind fences, horse troughs, rain barrels, and that antique pickup truck.

I led the gang toward the barn.

Suddenly, six screaming horses came stampeding toward us, all of them ridden by alien outlaw freaks who were spurring the stallions' ribs, hard.

"Time to dismount!" I commanded, swinging out my leg to roundhouse kick the lead rider off his steed.

On my right, I could see Willy leaping up into a flying back kick. Dana was going with a scissor kick, attempting to take down two riders at once.

But an instant before any of our blows landed, the

horses transformed into rocket bikes and zoomed away, torching our shins with their afterburners.

"Mel's not with them!" I shouted as I tumbled to the ground.

"The first bunch must've taken her," reported Willy. "I saw them morph into some kind of robots and shoot skyward. They were hauling a sealed capsule behind them."

That capsule had to be Mel's portable prison cell.

"Take these criminals down!" Agent Judge shouted to his team, and they immediately started firing. Hot tracers streaked through the sky. Warbling shock blasts rippled through the air. Unfortunately, when that last invader squeaked through the shrinking exit hole, the FBI weapon bursts ricocheted off the inner lining of my refurbished dome.

"Cease fire!" I shouted as boomeranging ammunition pummeled the ground around us. "Cease fire!"

Agent Judge took up the call. "Cease fire!"

We dodged the incoming blasts until the last of the deflected shots sprang back at us.

Then everything under the dome became incredibly, horribly quiet.

I looked over at Agent Judge. I've never seen a man look so shocked or grim.

"Don't worry, sir," I said. "I'm going after her."

Not yet, I heard Xanthos's voice say in my head. It was weak, barely audible. *Not . . . yet . . .*

He sounded like he was hurt.

No—it was worse.

It sounded like my spiritual advisor was dying.

Chapter 47

XANTHOS WAS LYING on his side in his stall. I could see that the straw scattered around his battered body had been scorched; his flowing white mane was singed and seared. I'm not certain what kind of flame-throwing weapons the thugs had used, but one thing was totally clear: they had come to these stables with orders to kill.

Xanthos was barely clinging to life. His blackened rib cage rose up and down very slowly, the movement accompanied by a wet death rattle creaking up from his lungs.

My brudda, I reached out mentally to my fallen friend.

Believe it or not, a slight grin twitched across his muzzle.

My brudda, he thought back.

What did those animals do to you?

The worst they could, Daniel. They live to hate. For this, we must pity them. For they will never know the one true love that unites us all.

Hang on. I can fix you.

No, Daniel. There are some things even you cannot repair.

I'm not going to let you die.

It is not your choice, brudda. We are all mortal. Otherwise, we would be gods, no? Fate has . . .

His voice grew fainter in my head.

Xanthos? I pleaded.

I could sense him mustering his final ounces of strength. *It is written in the book. . . .*

What is written? I asked.

He took a wheezy breath. *My destiny. Yours.*

What is my destiny?

To be true . . .

He was slipping away. His wide nostrils were barely fluttering.

To be true to what? I leaned closer.

To . . . who . . . you . . . truly . . . are . . .

And with that, there was nothing in my mind but my own mournful thoughts.

My spiritual advisor was dead.

I cradled his majestic head in my lap and rocked it back and forth. Tears stung my eyes and streamed down my cheeks.

Xanthos, an extremely gentle creature who'd never uttered a harsh word—not even for those who came here to kill him—had, in just a few short days, really worked his way deep into my soul. Now his death was rocking my world.

I don't think I've cried that hard in years.

And I didn't want to do it again for a long, long time. I didn't want Agent Judge doing it, either.

Another reason why I had to go rescue Mel— immediately!

Chapter 48

I GENTLY CLOSED Xanthos's soulful brown eyes.

As I did, I realized something: I killed him.

I also got Mel kidnapped.

If I had never come to Kentucky, if I had never met my father's spiritual advisor, if I hadn't gone horseback riding, if Xanthos hadn't bucked me off his back when we were crossing that creek, if...

"What're you doing, Daniel?"

It was Dana.

I gently laid Xanthos's head on a pillow of the cleanest straw I could scrape together in his stall. "He's dead," I said faintly. "I killed him."

"No, you didn't." Dana knelt down beside me and wiped the last tear from my eye. "You feel terrible about what happened to your friends. Maybe you even feel guilty, because if you weren't here, things wouldn't have gone down the way they did."

"Exactly."

"You're right, Daniel. If you weren't here, things would be different. In fact, they'd be a whole lot worse."

"No."

"Daniel, if you hadn't put that dome over our heads..."

"It didn't stop them."

"No. But it sure slowed them down. If you weren't here, chances are Number 2 would've wiped this horse farm off the map the same way he took down New York, Beijing, London, and Moscow. You saved Agent Judge's life, not to mention all those other FBI agents out there."

"But what about Mel?"

"She's a tough girl. She'll be fine."

"Wait a second. Are you actually saying something nice about Melody Judge?"

"Whoa. Don't get carried away...."

"But I think I just heard you actually compliment Mel."

Dana shrugged. "She's okay. I mean, for an earthling."

I actually brightened to hear her say it. "You like her, don't you?"

"Um, let's leave 'like' out of this, okay? Mel saved my bacon on the bridge. I figure I owe her one. So come on; let's go rescue her already. I don't like being in debt."

I reached out and held Dana's cheek in my hand so I could gaze into her brilliant blue eyes. "You're really something, Dana—you know that, right?"

"What?" she said with a laugh. "Are you admiring your own handiwork again?"

"Man, sometimes I *so* wish you were real."

"Yeah," she said sweetly. "Me, too."

As I cupped her cheek in my hand, I let my thumb trace the white line that was still marring her otherwise perfect skin.

"You like my souvenir?" Dana joked. "I picked it up in Moscow."

"I'm going to fix that, you know."

"I know. But first we need to fix the rest of this mess."

I was holding Dana's cheek, gazing into her eyes, which were steadily gazing back into mine. We were definitely having a moment.

A moment that was suddenly shattered by the roar of a thousand gunning helicopter engines hovering overhead.

Chapter 49

DANA AND I raced out of the barn.

"What's going on?" I called to Willy.

"Choppers. Hundreds of them."

"What about the dome?"

Joe shook his head. "They overrode whatever you cooked up." He was shouting to be heard over the din of the thumping rotors. "I can't explain it, but the dome has disappeared. Completely."

I shielded my eyes and glanced up at the sky. The stars were all gone, blotted out by the horde of hovering helicopters. The aircraft looked more like heavily armored dragonflies than conventional whirlybirds.

One helicopter drifted down from the pack and, swaying slightly, landed right in front of us, kicking up a funnel cloud of dust and straw.

A clamshell-style door opened on the side of the craft to reveal a set of stairs. A giant—maybe fifteen feet tall—descended the steps. He was dressed in princely robes, and his curly hair and beard writhed around his grotesque face as if they were twin nests of coiled snakes. When his leaden, size thirty-six boots touched the ground, the whole Earth shook.

The emissary beat his chest with his fist, then held up an open palm as if he were a Roman tribune.

"Grakkings, oodoo pooflee," he proclaimed. "Utoo a reschendedante Gogg. Ja reschendente atta ulti magno chimando e devoosheekmo gensei Abbadon."

The FBI agents and my gang had giant "Huh?" expressions etched on their faces.

Fortunately, my alien brain contains the equivalent of a universal translator. I can understand any creature speaking any language—including the languages they don't teach in any high school in the known universe.

"He says, 'Greetings, weak ones,'" I translated. "'I am Ambassador Gogg. I represent the almighty, ever-powerful, and all-destroying Lord Abbadon.'" *Even though he looks like he's on his way to a supersized toga party*, I thought.

While Gogg preened and waited for us to cower in fear before his towering magnificence, I stepped forward.

"Itchay umknock gensei Abbadon solto fracking 'ulti magno e chimando' que sempro no reschendente wimmish?"

"Huh?" muttered Joe.

"I said, 'If your so-called Lord Abbadon is so freaking 'almighty and powerful,' why is he afraid to represent himself?'"

"Nice, Daniel," said Dana. "Very diplomatic."

The giant plodded forward. "Vu diche nomin Daniel?"

"Yeah," I said. "That's my name. Don't wear it out. And, by the way, you're on Earth now. So speak English, French, Spanish, Chinese, Lithuanian—anything but that dreck that's dribbling out of your face-hole now."

"As you wish, weakling," Gogg said, haughtily raising his long, anteater-esque snout. "Tell me, Daniel: Do you miss your little pony?"

"Xanthos isn't gone." I tapped a hand to my heart. "He's still here."

Gogg raised a dainty paw to his nose nozzle. "Oh, my. Such sentimental claptrap. Tell me, do you miss your little friend Melody? Or is she still here, too?" He drummed his triple-jointed fingers in a paradiddle over his chest to mock me.

"If you harm one hair on Mel's head, I will personally destroy you ten seconds after I destroy Abbadon!"

He stopped his girlish giggles and got all huffy. "My, my, my. Such big, bold words."

"He can back those words up," shouted Dana. "Just ask anybody on The List of Alien Outlaws on Terra Firma."

"Yeah," said Joe. "Ask Attila. Or Number 3, that flaming burnout we extinguished in London."

"Ask numbers 6, 43, 40, or 19!" shouted Willy.

"Oh, wait," said Dana. "You can't ask any of them. Because Daniel's already done to them what he's going to do to you and your 'Lord' if you idiots don't do as you're told and bring back Mel!"

"Oh, Lord Abbadon is quite willing to set her free," said

Ambassador Gogg with a grin that sent his slippery snake beard squirming again. "In fact, I am here to parlay over the terms of her release."

Agent Judge had heard enough. He strode forward and stood by my side. "And what, exactly, does Abbadon want in exchange for my daughter?"

"Nothing much," said Gogg. "Just *him*."

And he flapped out a limb to point at me.

Chapter 50

AMBASSADOR GOGG FLICKED his wrist and a glowing holographic scroll appeared in the misty air beside him. As the diplomatic cable unfurled, two words in neon green jumped out of the illuminated legal mumbo jumbo: DANIEL X.

"As I stated," said Gogg, "the terms of the agreement are quite simple. Her life for yours. The party of the first part, in exchange for certain..."

My universal translator decoded his next several chunks of legalese as "Blah, blah, blah. Yadda, yadda, yadda." But while the giant babbled, I had time to consider how to take down the whole armada. But the "blah, blah, blahs" in my head became real words again soon because my brain knew I needed to hear this:

"And, to prevent the party of the second part, Daniel X, from initiating any of his customary parlor tricks against my duly appointed diplomatic representative and said diplomat's military escort, be advised that the captive, one

Melody Judge, will be dealt with most harshly should any treachery befall my messenger and/or airships."

Gogg looked up and, in a blinding flash, every one of the two hundred helicopters flipped on high-intensity spotlights mounted to their undercarriages. The lights were actually incredibly bright LCD projectors, which blasted the ground around us with hi-def video images of Mel, sitting in a straight-back chair, her wrists and ankles bound with heavy chains. A dozen weapon-toting aliens surrounded her.

In other words, if I cooked up a counterstrike, Mel would be struck dead.

At my side, Agent Judge was about to drop to his knees to be closer to the images shimmering on the ground all around us.

I braced him by the elbow. "Don't let them see how much it hurts, sir. They'll just use it against you. Against her."

Agent Judge nodded and stiffened his spine.

"At least we know she's okay," I whispered.

"But how long will she stay that way?"

"Until Number 2 gets what he really wants: me."

"Well, Daniel?" boomed Gogg. "Do you agree to my Lord's extremely generous terms?"

I looked at Agent Judge. He was shaking his head. "No. I can't let you do this. You're too valuable. You're this planet's last and best hope."

Gogg heaved an aggravated sigh, like we were boring him, and said, "Might I remind you, Daniel, that if we don't hear what we're *dying* to hear, someone else will be dying, very soon?"

He gestured grandly toward the ground and the two hundred projections of Mel surrounded by Abbadon's heavily armed henchbeasts. The aliens raised their weapons. Took aim. It was a circular firing squad, with Mel in the middle.

I had to give Number 2's ambassador an answer. Now.

And it had to be the *right* answer!

There would be absolutely no makeups on this exam.

Chapter 51

"FINE," I ANNOUNCED. "Tell your Lord and Master that he can have me."

"No, Daniel," said Agent Judge. "I will not let you trade your life for Mel's!"

"I'm playing a hunch, sir," I whispered tersely.

"No," he said again, ignoring me and shouting directly up to the giant Gogg. "You cannot have Daniel. Do I make myself clear, sir?"

"Extremely." Gogg flicked open a large ring on the third knuckle of his pinkie finger and brought the thing up toward the fluttering tip of his snout.

"Wait!" I cried out.

Clearly the pinkie ring was some kind of communicator, and he was about to call in the order for Mel's execution.

"Hang on another second," I said. "Let Agent Judge and me hash this out."

"No, Daniel," said Agent Judge, even though I could tell

that saying no to me and yes to his daughter's execution was tearing him apart. "I will not permit you to lose your life! Too many other lives hang in the balance."

I circled my finger near my temple to let Gogg know I thought Agent Judge was acting crazy. "Um, he and I need to chat," I said as pleasantly as I could, so that Gogg would think I was on his side.

"Fine," said Gogg. "You have one Earth minute."

I grabbed Agent Judge and spun him around so Gogg couldn't hear what we were saying—or read our lips.

"Don't worry," I said as quickly as I could. "I'm calling his bluff."

"Daniel, as much as I admire your courage, as much as I want you to save Mel's life, the good of the many outweighs the good of the few, or the one."

"But if my hunch is correct, we won't lose the many, the few, or, most important, the one." I motioned toward the images of Mel fearlessly facing her firing squad. Never flinching. Never letting her enemy see how terrified she must truly be.

"What are you thinking, Daniel?"

"That, for some reason I haven't figured out yet, Abbadon is afraid of me."

Agent Judge arched an eyebrow. "And what makes you say that?"

"In New York City, before he decked me with that sucker punch and sent me sailing into the future, he could've killed me. He could've come after me himself outside that coal mine in West Virginia, but he sent Attila.

When he decimated D.C., he didn't come to destroy us; he just put a price on my head. And tonight? If it was so easy for his troops to penetrate our defenses, why didn't Number 2 come along for the ride? Why did he send this emissary?"

"You raise some very interesting questions, Daniel...."

"I don't think Abbadon will harm Mel until he gets me exactly where he wants me—wherever that might be."

"Go with your gut, son," said Agent Judge. "I'll back you up all the way."

I nodded and we both turned around to face Gogg once again.

"Okay, Ambassador Gogg. Tell your boss he can have what he wants. He can have me."

"Wonderful," purred the giant idiot. "Abbadon will be most pleased. You will kindly enter my vessel and—"

"No. We do this thing right here, right now."

"B-b-but—"

"This whole horse farm can be our arena. He sends away the helicopters, I tell my FBI guys to take a hike. It's just him and me. One-on-one. Winner takes all. Including, of course, Miss Melody Judge."

"I, uh..."

"What's Abbadon afraid of?"

Gogg nervously wiggled his gangly fingers and thought long and hard about what he could say into that pinkie-ring communicator that wouldn't incur Abbadon's wrath.

I was right. Number 2 didn't want to tangle with me in New York, Moscow, London, Beijing, or even Kentucky because he *needed* our battle to take place somewhere else, maybe even some*time* else.

Why?

I had no earthly idea.

Chapter 52

WHILE GOGG FRETTED and wiggled his articulated digits, all the images of Mel instantly dissolved into an extreme (and extremely ugly) close-up of Number 2.

I was instantly overcome by a severe case of the heebie-jeebies. Number 2's appearance in the projections was different from the other guises I had already seen him put on. Now he had his face slathered with brightly colored war paint, like William Wallace and his Highlanders in that movie *Braveheart.* Of course, I knew it was Number 2, no matter how much makeup he put on. His glowing-ember eyes totally gave him away.

"Hello again, Daniel."

"Hello, Abbadon. Long time, no see."

"Yes. What a shame you had to leave New York without seeing the Statue of Liberty—facedown and drowning in the harbor."

"She won't stay that way for long."

"Is that a threat?"

I shrugged. "More like a promise."

"You think *you* can undo what *I* have done?"

"Sure. And the humans who built the statue in the first place will help."

"Oh, yes. Earthlings can be quite helpful when they support one's cause. Oh, by the way, Daniel—did you enjoy your time in Tomorrowland?"

"It was fantastic. Mostly because *you* weren't there."

"Is that so?"

"Yeah. A guy named Bob told me you had scurried underground to hide in your rat hole."

"True. Because you see, Daniel, by tomorrow, under-ground is where Mel will be. With me. In fact, while you were wasting time, stumbling about in the future, the love of your life had already spent a dozen hours as my prisoner in the underworld."

I quickly glanced over at Dana.

She had her game face on; Number 2's little dig about Mel being the "love of my life" hadn't fazed her in the least.

"Tell me, Daniel," Abbadon asked, his voice soft and provocative, "had you ever done that before? Had you ever flown *forward* through time?"

I gave him another shrug. "Never really wanted to. Because, unlike the past, the future is extremely change-able. You never really know what tomorrow may bring, even if you've already been there."

"Bravo, Daniel," he said with a smile. "Finally you prove yourself a nimble thinker and, perhaps, a worthy adversary. Soon all will be as it was always meant to be! To the victor shall go *all* the spoils, including your young lady friend."

"You're not just going to kill her while no one is watching?"

"Of course not. Where's the sport in that? I want you to be here when she dies."

I didn't answer him, because I didn't want to say something stupid that might jeopardize Mel's safety. As it stood, she'd stay alive until Abbadon and I finally did battle — wherever and whenever he needed that smackdown to take place.

"By the way," Number 2 continued, "while you and Bob were wasting your tomorrow, I was busy amassing my troops to wipe out all those who dared resist my initial invitation to join me in the underworld."

Now the multiple images of Abbadon were replaced by footage of massive armies on the march.

"Gaze upon another glimpse of the future, Daniel!"

The troops rolling forward under Abbadon's black banner were a motley assortment of alien outlaws in full combat gear. They had battle drones, robo-tanks, and laser-guided missile launchers. They also had something that totally chilled me to the bone: human allies.

Number 2 smiled, a thin grin crackling across his painted lips. "As I said before, Daniel, these humans can be so very helpful when they find a cause they truly believe in!"

As I stared down in disbelief at the human mercenaries

who had taken on Abbadon's fight, I heard him hiss, "Come to me and save your lady fair!"

And then the two hundred projector beams went black.

The helicopters disappeared from the sky.

Even the mincing Ambassador Gogg was gone.

"How'd he do that?" said Joe, totally perplexed.

"Very well," mumbled Emma, in a faint echo of what she usually said whenever *I* pulled off some impossibly spectacular transformation.

"We bought some time," said Agent Judge. "Abbadon clearly wants the home-field advantage when you two go head-to-head. Any reason why?"

"No, sir. In fact, all I know for sure is that, right now, Mel is safe."

And, for Agent Judge and me, that was really all that mattered.

Chapter 53

"THE HOUSE IS huge, ladies and gentlemen," Agent Judge said to the five of us after a long postmortem on the night's incredibly hair-raising events. "Pick a bedroom and hit the rack. All of you. Especially you, Daniel." He had learned that my creative powers get totally zonked when I don't get to recharge my battery.

I grabbed a bedroom on the second floor. The rest of the gang didn't really need to find rooms or, for that matter, go to sleep. It was one of the bonus features of being a product of my imagination: when I powered down, they did, too.

I closed my eyes.

When I did, just for an instant, I saw Mel, tied up in that chair.

"Hold on," I whispered. "I'm coming."

Right before I drifted off to sleep, my dream girl smiled back and said, "Don't worry, Daniel." She playfully jostled her chains. "I'm not going anywhere. I'm sort of tied up at the moment."

Believe it or not, after all that had happened, I actually fell asleep with a smile on my face.

A smile that disappeared maybe three hours later, when I woke with a start.

My super alien ears had heard a floorboard creak while I was asleep and sent a signal to my brain saying *This is not good.*

Someone was in the house.

Sneaking around. Trying to not make a sound.

Now the someone was in my bedroom.

Moving closer to the bed.

It had to be Number 2. All that talk about meeting him on his turf? Another trick from the great deceiver, an attempt to lull me into thinking I could lower my guard for an instant and catch some shut-eye.

Well, two could play that game.

I'd trick *him* into thinking I was still asleep.

I kept my eyes closed and summoned up every ounce of my level-three strength. I was ready to rumble.

I heard another board squeak and my brain did a quick sonar ping. The intruder was very close, almost on top of me.

Fine. This bedroom would be our final battlefield.

I would fight Number 2 to the death, right here, right now!

Chapter 54

A SPLIT SECOND before Number 2 leaped in for the kill, I sprang up out of bed and attacked him.

I went at him with a double haymaker. Both of my arms whipped sideways with the slightest bend at the elbows and met his head smack in the center. It was pitch dark in the room, so I couldn't see the look of shock on Abbadon's face when both my fists slammed into his temples. I imagined his blood-red eyeballs must've nearly popped out of their sockets.

I activated my night-vision ocular lenses (they're just another handy feature of my Alpar Nokian anatomy) so I wouldn't be fighting totally blind. At least I now had a greenish-gray blob to target.

But as I was lining up my next blow, the blob came down at me with a hammer fist to my head.

I tucked and rolled off the bed and immediately jumped up into a flying scissor kick. Locking my legs around my attacker's torso, I twisted sideways in midair and took him down, hard.

When the intruder hit the deck, he wrapped his arms around my legs and yanked me down to the floor with him. Then, bouncing up to his feet, he grabbed me by my ankles so he could spin me around and around like I was his figure-skating partner and he was going to neatly dump me on the ice in an elegant death spiral.

Before he could let go and send me sailing, I fought against the centrifugal force as he swung me around in a dizzying circle and sat up in midair by executing the most amazing abdominal crunch I have ever grunted through. When I was in a locked and upright position, I gave him another double wallop to both sides of his skull.

"Blows to the head are illegal!" my attacker shouted through his pain.

I was too shocked to land another hit. I flopped out of the sit-up. My arms fell limply to my sides.

"Dad?"

"Never lower your guard, son!"

He let go of my ankles and sent me flying into the far wall. I slammed into it so hard I shattered a couple of picture frames, slid down fast, and crash-landed with a bang on my butt.

"Gravity," said my attacker. "It's always putting people down."

Yep. It was definitely my father. I recognized his penchant for corny puns.

Just so we're clear, as I've already told you, my real parents are dead thanks to The Prayer, the mantis-looking freak who still holds the number one spot on The List Of Alien Outlaws on Terra Firma, as well as on the unofficial Daniel X List of Creeps in Serious Need of Extermination. My imagined parents are probably just mental projections built on a neural framework of memories and sensory recall, but when I manifest my dad, he's as real as you or me. His punches, kicks, and body blows are extremely real, too.

He always shows up exactly when I need him most.

See, I don't need to *summon* my father. Some part of my brain (maybe way down deep in its fight-or-flight reptilian stem) knows when I need some serious parental guidance. Call it my survival instinct.

"So," my father said, rubbing his temples, where I could see (now that he had removed whatever blackout blinds he'd materialized over the bedroom windows) two red welts rising where my knuckles had collided with his cranium. "You let me get the drop on you, but you think you're ready to take on Number 2?"

"I have to, Dad. He's destroying the entire planet. Plus, he nabbed Agent Judge's daughter. You remember Agent Judge?"

"Yes, Daniel. Martin Judge was a good friend to your mother and me. And I know all about what Number 2 is up to, how he kidnapped Melody. Xanthos filled me in on everything."

"What?"

"My former spiritual advisor and I were recently reunited. Right after his immortal soul slipped free of his lifeless body."

"I'm so sorry, Dad. I didn't mean to get him killed."

"You didn't, son. It was his time. His destiny. Just like it was *your* destiny to finally meet up with my wise old friend. I hope you're doing everything Xanthos advised you to do."

I lowered my eyes. "I'm trying."

"Good. Now it's my turn. I'll help you get ready to battle Number 2."

I looked around the room. "Does Mom know you're here?"

"Yes, Daniel. Reluctantly, she agrees: I must do everything I can to prepare you for what is guaranteed to be the fight of your life."

"The two of us against all of them?"

"No, *just you*, Daniel."

"Solo?" I asked my dad, even though I obviously knew the answer. He nodded. "But...his army is even bigger than I first feared when I tracked him to that cave in West Virginia," I couldn't help saying. "He has a legion of alien lackeys, plus thousands—maybe millions—of humans who have actually deserted their brothers and sisters to fight for him!"

"It's your destiny," he reminded me. "I'll help you become a better, smarter, more imaginative warrior. I'll teach you everything I can in the short time we have left."

"How can Number 2 be the one who destroys this

planet?" I asked. "How can this second-ranked alien hope to accomplish what the top dog, Number 1, never could?"

"Because he has *their* help."

"The humans? The ones taking his side in this war?"

My father nodded knowingly, and I flashed back to my first encounter with Number 2, down in that West Virginia cavern. *This planet is ripe for the taking*, the demon had boasted to his loyal followers. *The human race has never been more divided, more shortsighted, more consumed with greed, or more inflamed by religious differences.*

Talk about a weird twist.

The humans that my father, my mother, and I had come to this planet to protect might just be the ones who ended up handing it over to the evil aliens!

Chapter 55

MY FATHER AND I left the house and headed into the barn. Somehow, even though Xanthos was dead, his calming spirit seemed to linger in the air, making his horse crib an ideal place to concentrate.

Dad was in total sensei mode. "You must master the mixed forms of martial arts, Daniel."

"I already have. Karate, tae kwon do, jeet kune, Brazilian jujitsu."

"Really?" said my father, circling me. "You know all the moves? All the rules?"

"Yes," I said, following him with a wary eye. "After all, you're the one who—"

My father leaped into the most vicious kick he's ever aimed at me. When his foot hit my groin, I doubled over in pain, which meant I gave him a great target for a fists-locked double uppercut to my chin.

I could taste blood; I'd bitten my tongue.

"There is only one rule when fighting Number 2, Daniel."

"What is it?"

"There are no rules!"

He pounced on me again.

I slammed up both my arms to block his blows.

"Good, Daniel," my father said as he used the momentum from my counterstrike to roll into a backward somersault and land in a crouching-tiger position. "But not good enough!"

This time his foot flew in a whirling windmill kick to my face.

This was cage fighting without the cage. And I would need every kick, punch, and combination I could come up with.

Because my father was trying to kill me.

Literally.

He leaped into the air, scissor-wrapped his legs around my neck, and slammed me down to the ground. One second before my skull hit a rock, I countered with a grunting head roll that brought his ankle down on the boulder instead.

Dad screamed in agony when his bone snapped.

Free from his leg hold, I sprang up into a star jump just as he spiraled into a flying twin-knuckle *tsuki* that socked me in the stomach so hard I thought my lungs would never hold air again.

Clearly, he had completely recovered from his ankle fracture.

"Overconfidence will kill you, son."

No. My *father* was going to kill me!

Revved up on adrenaline, I flew into a fight frenzy.

My father and I exchanged a wicked series of blows and counter blows, kicks and counter kicks.

And then we tried to strangle each other.

This went on for at least an hour. A couple of my ribs felt as if they'd splintered like chicken bones. My legs were turning to rubber from sheer exhaustion and the drain of all that adrenaline. And my father wasn't letting up.

Now that I knew he was definitely trying to kill me, I decided it was time to return the favor.

"Be careful, son," he taunted as he swaggered around me. "Focus. Fight with your head."

"Thanks for the suggestion!" I said, hurtling at his gut headfirst, like a battering ram.

But my father became a matador outwitting a charging bull and sidestepped me before I made impact. For good measure, he fist-jabbed me hard in both kidneys as I breezed past his hip.

Dazed and totally embarrassed, I could feel the rage rising up through my neck to scorch the tips of my ears.

"Do not give sway to the negative way," said my father.

I guess he learned that little ditty from Xanthos, back in the day.

I couldn't care less. My father was the one who had dragged me into this mess in the first place. He was the one dumb enough to let Number 1 get the drop on him, and then he did absolutely *nothing* to save my mom. It was my father's fault that I ended up an orphan, and then what did he do? He left me my inheritance—the stupid List, plus the ridiculous mission to protect an entire planet from all sorts of creeped-out alien invaders, even though I was only a kid. Which, I have to say, seriously screwed me up. Wouldn't it screw *you* up? Heck, I couldn't even have a girlfriend without her getting kidnapped by drooling interplanetary delinquents. And to add insult to injury, every now and then, just for chuckles, my father seemed to pop back into my world so he could boss me around and kick the crap out of me.

So, here and now, all I wanted was to kill my deadbeat dad for all he had done to me. Like ruining my life.

Yeah, I seriously wanted to kill the guy. I wanted to finish this whole stupid Alien Hunter thing right here, right now.

My father relaxed his fists and let his arms hang loosely at his sides.

"I recognize that look in your eye, Daniel."

"What about it?"

"It is hate, pure and simple. Hate fueled by rage."

"So?"

"Making his targets slaves to hate is how Abbadon wins, son. It is how he has *always* won."

Chapter 56

MY FATHER TRANSFORMED the walls of the barn into movie screens onto which he projected a series of extremely graphic and grisly scenes, all of them rated H for Horrible and Horrifying.

And Historical.

Genghis Khan and his Mongol hordes devastating Central Asia and Russia.

King Herod the Great ordering the execution of all the young male children in the village of Bethlehem so he wouldn't lose his throne to the "king" whose birth three wise men had read in the stars.

The horrors and tortures of the Spanish Inquisition, including the burning at the stake of all those whom the church declared heretics.

Robespierre and his Reign of Terror. Sixteen thousand people losing their heads to the guillotine.

King Leopold of Belgium's atrocities in the Congo.

The murders of the Romanov family by the Bolsheviks in Russia in 1918.

The mass murder of many millions of people in the Soviet Union under Lenin and Stalin.

"Do you see him, Daniel?" my father asked as we watched Nazi soldiers wiping out the Warsaw Ghetto in 1941.

"No."

"Look carefully. There. Skulking in the background."

I stared beyond the hate-filled Nazis and the terrified Jews, and saw two glowing red dots.

I looked harder.

I saw him. The two points of throbbing red were his hideous, burning eyes.

"It's Number 2! He was there?"

My father nodded. "Throughout history, whenever humankind, fueled by ignorance and hate, turns against itself, you will see him."

And I did. Now that I knew what I was looking for, Abbadon was easy to spot. His appearance always changed, but his eyes never did. They burned like stoked embers in a hearth under the blast of a bellows whenever humans committed atrocities against other humans.

At the Jallianwala Bagh massacre of unarmed Indian protestors by the British in 1919.

In the killing fields of Cambodia, when the Marxist Khmer Rouge regime murdered more than two million of its fellow Cambodians.

He was there when Saddam Hussein gassed the Kurds.

He gloried in Beijing's Tiananmen Square massacre in 1989.

He cheered on the holocaust in Rwanda when a million Tutsis were butchered.

"He is always there," my father said. "He triumphs when hatred overpowers all other human emotions. Study him, Daniel. Study everything he does—and I mean everything. Every movement, every gesture, every telling smile. Look for his weaknesses."

"I don't see any!"

"Look harder."

I did, but all I saw was the crimson-eyed fiend lurking in the background, delighting as human beings turned on one another. I watched until I couldn't watch anymore.

I turned my head away from the carnage flowing across the barn walls just as Colonel Gaddafi was sending foreign mercenaries into the streets of Tripoli to murder his fellow Libyans.

"Focus, Daniel! Focus!"

I refused to look at the horror displayed on the walls any longer.

"Who is this monster?" I demanded.

"Focus, son!"

"No. Tell me. The List can't, but you can, can't you? *Who is Number 2?*"

My father heaved the heaviest sigh I have ever heard in my life.

"Very well, Daniel. You leave me no choice."

I couldn't believe it: my father was finally ready to tell me *everything*!

Chapter 57

MY FATHER'S FINAL lesson for the day was a shocker.

"This was the battle *I* had been preparing for, Daniel. In Kansas."

"When Number 1 came for you and Mom?"

My father nodded.

"But why were you training to fight Number 2? Why not Number 1? If you had concentrated on the top gun..."

"It was my mission, Daniel. It was why your mother and I came to this planet."

"To fight Number 2? I don't get it."

"Daniel, Number 2 is the one humans call the Prince of Darkness. He is Satan."

"The devil?"

Now the walls of the barn were filled with fiery images. Michelangelo's fresco *The Last Judgment* from the altar wall of the Sistine Chapel, showing Satan as the boatman Charon ferrying the evildoers down to hell. A snake hissing in the verdant undergrowth of a garden. The cloven-hoofed, twin-horned fiend of legend and horror films.

My father turned to gaze at the devilish imagery writhing across the walls.

"He is the great pretender," my father said. "A fallen angel fighting for souls, hoping to lure them into the darkness. He is the one Muslims call Iblis, a demon created out of smokeless fire. He is Beelzebub, who can cast evil suggestions into the hearts of men and women. He is the one ancient Zoroastrians called Angra Mainyu, 'the destructive spirit.' And you, Daniel, must fight him."

"Why?"

"Because this is the beginning of the Apocalypse. The final, cataclysmic battle between the forces of good and the forces of evil; the ultimate struggle between the creator and the destroyer; a clash that is written about in holy texts on every planet in this universe because the devil — the one who thrives on evil, hatred, and destruction — is everywhere."

"Wait a second," I said. "If Number 2 is the devil, who or *what* is Number 1?"

"Something much worse," said my father. "He is a deity, Daniel. *A god.*"

PART THREE

WELCOME TO THE APOCALYPSE

Chapter 58

WHEN I WOKE up, I smelled pancakes. It was quite a contrast to the horrors I'd learned about the night before from Dad.

I rolled out of the bed in the Judges' guest room and made my way downstairs to the kitchen.

I was relieved to see that the walls in Agent Judge's house displayed the usual sort of framed pictures—not the horror show I had witnessed when my father turned the walls of the barn into the multiplex from hell. But seeing so many pictures of Mel—riding a pony in the paddock, winning her first horse-show ribbon, crossing *our* creek on horseback—bummed me out nearly as much.

Mel was still missing, of course.

And now I knew who had her: the devil himself. Going down the list of baddies you could be kidnapped by, it doesn't get much worse than that.

I stepped into the kitchen.

"Good morning, Daniel."

It was my mother, cooking up a storm. Like my dad, she is a total manifestation of my imagination and shares his uncanny ability to show up exactly when I need her most. And, like most moms, she also knows exactly what to make for breakfast when life gets tough. In addition to the pancakes I had already sniffed out, there were a dozen eggs sputtering in a skillet; bacon, sausage, and ham sizzling on the grill; cheese grits simmering in a pot; biscuits and cinnamon buns in the oven; pitchers of juice (orange, apple, grape, and grapefruit); and, of course, toast.

Hey, it's just not breakfast without toast.

"Erm, are we expecting company?"

"No, dear. This is all for you. Your warrior's breakfast."

It's a tradition in cultures everywhere: Before you go off to do battle, you pig out with one last feast. Either that or you fast in the desert to give yourself a lean, mean edge. Personally, I prefer the feast to the fast.

I settled in at the kitchen table and secured a checkered napkin in the collar of my T-shirt. Then I tucked into the mountain of food Mom had piled on my plate. When I was halfway through my second stack of pancakes, my mother sat down at the table with me.

"Daniel, do you know why your father never did battle with Number 2?"

"I guess because I was like three years old and he didn't want to risk losing his death match with the devil, which would leave *you* a single parent and *me* a fatherless child.

Of course, the way things worked out, I turned into a total orphan instead."

My mother smiled and shook her head. "That's not why he refused the fight, Daniel."

I put down my knife and fork. She reached across the table to touch my hand with hers.

"Going up against the devil is not a task to be taken lightly. You only get one chance. If you lose, the consequences are dire."

"Wasn't Dad ready? Was he afraid?"

"Your father has not been afraid of anything or anyone since the time he was two years old and his mother accidentally dropped him in the middle of an elephant stampede during mastodon mating season."

"So why didn't he take down Number 2 when he had the chance?"

"Because he knew a stronger warrior was coming along. One better suited to the task than he."

"Who?"

"You, Daniel. You have more powers than your father and I combined. You are the one whose destiny has always been to deal with Number 2. I sometimes think creating *you* was the reason fate decreed that your father and I fall in love. Now we need to pray that you are ready for this fight."

Then, right there at the kitchen table, my mom and I locked hands and bowed our heads to pray.

Hey, if you go up against evil alien baddies on a regular

basis, prayer can be extremely useful. Sometimes you just need to call on a power greater than yourself—even if you, yourself, have all kinds of great powers.

But I never prayed like this before. And my mother? Her intensity was off the charts.

When we were finished I couldn't help but ask, "Why did you pray so hard, Mom?"

"I'm trying to prepare you—and me—for the possibility of your death."

"You think I'm gonna die when I go up against Abbadon?"

"Death is always with us, Daniel. None of us is immortal. Eventually, we must all depart this realm and move on to the next."

Okay, even after biscuits and slabs of ham, that was probably the heaviest thing my mom could have served me for breakfast. And she wasn't finished.

"Someone close to my heart is going to die soon, Daniel. I can feel it. The feeling is so strong there is an aura of certainty surrounding it."

Something else you should probably know about my mom?

Her "feelings" are never, ever wrong.

Chapter 59

"GOOD MORNING, DANIEL," Agent Judge greeted me as I entered the barnyard. "Sleep okay?"

"Yeah," I lied, deciding not to go into the bit about fighting my dad nearly to the death.

"You hungry? The cook set up a mess tent in the paddock."

"No thanks. I'm good."

"Okay, then." Agent Judge looked impatient. "We need to move out. Now. It's time to take the fight to Abbadon."

"Yes, sir. I was thinking we should double back to that abandoned coal mine in West Virginia. The bat cave might be some kind of an entrance into the underworld where he's holding Mel hostage."

I had decided not to tell Agent Judge what my father had told me—that this underworld might be *the* underworld, as in "the fiery pits of hell."

"I've put together a special strike force," Agent Judge continued. "Navy SEALs, Delta Force, Night Stalkers,

Special Forces, Rangers. They're the best of the best, Daniel. The bravest of the brave."

"Did somebody call my name?" said Willy as he strode confidently into the barnyard. Joe, Emma, and Dana came striding right behind him. "Hey, you said you wanted the best of the best and the bravest of the brave. Guess it's a good thing we were in the neighborhood, bro."

I had to grin. If I was about to head down to the gates of hell, I figured it'd be great to have my gang covering my back.

"Thanks for being here, guys. This could be our most important alien hunt ever. It could also be the most dangerous."

"Awesome," said Joe, sniffing the air. "So, is that bacon or sausage?"

"Both. Plus ham. Go grab some. But hurry. We need to move out."

"Grab some fruit, too, Joe," suggested Emma.

"Yeah, right. Like that's gonna happen."

"Meet us in the paddock with the strike force," I said.

"Will do."

Joe bounded into the house while the rest of us hustled over to meet the team Agent Judge had assembled.

About 150 warriors were milling about in the fenced-in corral, packing up their equipment and rations. These battle-hardened veterans were decked out in black tactical gear, gloves, boots, and helmets. Confiscated alien weapons and ammo belts were slung over their shoulders. Their game-day faces were hidden behind ski masks, goggles, and blackout paint.

Still, even with this outstanding strike force, I could not imagine how we could defeat an enemy as powerful as the devil.

And, as you already know, if I can't *imagine* it, I can't *do* it.

Chapter 60

"GENTLEMEN," I ANNOUNCED to the assembled troops, "my name is Daniel, and I will be your team leader on this mission."

One hundred and fifty pairs of eyeballs drilled into me.

"Please forgive me for what I'm sure sounds like foolish arrogance, but trust me: I need to take point on this operation."

The squadron of black-clad, armored warriors stood in stony silence.

"We are going up against an enemy unlike any you have ever encountered. As Agent Judge undoubtedly told you in his briefing, the monstrous warlord who calls himself Abbadon is an alien outlaw from an unknown planet and galaxy. What Agent Judge may not have told you is that I, too, am an alien. Over the past several years, I have dealt with and eliminated similar extraterrestrial threats to your planet. Therefore, I urge you not to let my youth mislead you. Yes, I am young, but right now, age is unimportant. I am the individual best suited to lead Earth's response to this specific threat."

I heard boots crinkle and weapons jangle as the soldiers shifted their weight from foot to foot while they considered my argument. Then one man stepped forward defiantly. He tipped up his goggles so I could read the steely machismo in his eyes.

"Prove it, kid," he snarled.

"Sir," I said firmly but (channeling my inner Xanthos) calmly, "we don't really have time to—"

"To what? To see if you're fit to lead?"

"Stand down, Navy SEAL," said Agent Judge.

"No, sir. I will not stand down, nor will I remain silent, because, frankly, I don't want to see more of my buddies die because some kid from outer space thinks he can become our field commander when he's not even old enough to legally enlist. Sorry, sir, but I'm not going into a firefight following someone who looks like he ought to be bagging my groceries."

Okay, the guy had a point. I was a kid. He was a professional. If I were him, would I follow me (or any other teenager) into a battle where the odds were so stacked against us? Doubtful. Unless, of course, the kid showed me that he (or she) was made of the right stuff. Then I might do it. Hey, Joan of Arc was a teenager when she led the French army to victory.

Macho Man swaggered forward, peeling off his weaponry and ammo belts. "You talk the talk, son. But can you walk the walk?" He tugged off his battle gloves, tucked

James Patterson

them into his helmet, and tossed the bundle to the side. "Why don't you show me what you've got?"

This SEAL was challenging me to a fight.

"Sir," I said, "we need every member of this squad in top physical condition when we go up against Abbadon. We can't afford casualties before we even encounter the enemy."

"Casualties?" Macho Man didn't like the sound of that.

"With all due respect, sir, I have no desire to hurt you."

"Whoo-ooh," the other soldiers jeered as they started to circle around us in the horse pen.

"Well, aren't you polite." The tough guy shed his tactical jacket. He was down to dog tags and a muscleman T-shirt. "Don't worry, son. I think I can handle anything you can dish out. Heck, kid, I've got underwear older than you."

"Daniel?" said Emma. "You could seriously hurt this human."

"Don't worry, Emma," I said. "I promise I won't throw a single punch."

"That's right, kid," said the SEAL. "Because I'm gonna take you down with one punch. Nighty-night, Danny Boy. It's lights-out time."

And with that, the toughest Navy SEAL in the bunch came at me with a wicked left hook.

Chapter 61

I IMMEDIATELY WHIPPED back my head.

Remember how fast I can run?

Well, my individual body parts can bob and weave at hyperspeed, too.

When the SEAL's fist sailed past the point where he thought my face should be, all he saw was a flesh-colored blur. So he tried again, this time with a right hook.

On the second punch, I think my head whooshing out of the way gave his knuckles windburn.

So he tried kicking me.

I dodged right.

He fell on his butt.

When he recovered and came at me with a second, soccer-style kick, I leaped up and landed behind him before he'd even completed his follow-through. His head swung back and forth a few times as he tried to figure out where I'd gone.

I tapped him on the shoulder to help him out. "Back here, sir."

He spun around.

"Stand still, kid."

"Not a wise strategy, sir."

He came at me with both hands, trying to throttle me.

I ducked down into a squat so fast that I swirled up a dust cloud like the Tasmanian Devil.

The SEAL nearly shattered his fingers when his hands locked in the space my neck had occupied a split second earlier.

"I'm gonna rip your heart out of your chest and show it to you while it's still beating, boy!"

Okay, I may have been the teenager in this fight, but the twentysomething SEAL could definitely win a medal for Most Immature. He was driven by sheer rage and kept flailing at me even as I zipped and zoomed out of reach.

"Fight me, kid!"

"I am!"

Hey, there's no rule that says you must always beat your opponent with brute force. Sometimes you can just wait him out and wear him down. Call it my siege strategy—a prolonged and persistent effort that weakens the enemy to the point of ultimate surrender. Yes, I could've transformed myself into a brick wall and let Mr. Machismo land one punch that would've shattered every spindly bone in his fist, but, like I said, we needed every soldier and sailor we could muster to go up against Abbadon.

The Navy SEAL was as tough as he looked. He kept coming at me. For a full hour.

Most of the other soldiers got bored with our zero-contact pas de deux. I saw Dana yawn. Joe went back into the kitchen for a second helping of bacon, sausage, and ham, taking a couple of Black Ops guys with him.

Finally, after an hour and sixteen minutes (I'm guessing a world record for a boxing match with *zero* points scored), the Navy SEAL — drenched in sweat and gasping for breath — collapsed in a crumpled heap on the ground.

"Emma?" I called out. She was, once again, geared up to be our company medic.

She rushed over to the fallen SEAL with a canteen full of Orange Elephant, the much more potent (and pungent) Alpar Nokian version of Red Bull. Two sips and you're totally revitalized.

One sip is all it takes if you're human.

"Outstanding, Daniel," the Navy SEAL conceded when the Orange Elephant kicked in and he remembered how his legs worked. "I'm impressed. The name's Lieutenant Russell," he said, thrusting out his right hand. "You lead. I'll follow. Heck, kid — I'd follow you into hell itself."

"Good," I said, grasping his hand firmly in mine. "Because that's exactly where we're going."

Chapter 62

A FLEET OF helicopters landed in the nearby pasture.

"Where'd those come from?" asked Agent Judge.

"Just something I whipped up so the strike force can hop over to West Virginia," I explained.

"Excellent. Where are the pilots?"

"We don't need them. I just need to imagine where you're going and the airships will fly you there."

The troops ducked under the rotor wash and carried their gear into the waiting choppers.

"*You* got us the birds?" Lieutenant Russell asked as he gathered up all the gear he had shed to fight me.

"Roger that," I said. "I figure a true leader needs to do more than duck punches."

He nodded. "See you in hell, sir," he said as he dashed off to hop into a chopper.

"Grab a helicopter, sir," I said to Agent Judge.

"I'll fly with you."

I shook my head. "I'm afraid you can't."

"Come again?"

"I'm going to teleport. I need to get there first to set up a landing beacon outside the cave entrance."

"Daniel?"

"Sir?"

"You wait for us. Don't you dare try to take on Number 2 by yourself."

"I won't, sir. A team leader is nothing without his team."

He shot me a salute. "See you in West Virginia."

While he raced off to a waiting whirlybird, I focused on the coordinates my internal GPS memory had locked in on when I logged the death of Number 33 (Attila) on The List. Traveling back to West Virginia, I wondered if the state should change the slogan on their license plates from ALMOST HEAVEN to JUST OUTSIDE HELL.

Chapter 63

WHEN I ARRIVED at my destination, my father was already there, waiting for me.

"Impressive technique, Daniel."

I thought he was commenting on my increasing skill at teleportation. "Thanks. Fortunately, I remember this place very vividly. It helped me fully grok the location."

Hey, it's hard to forget the place where you turned yourself into yak stew so you could work your way through an alien's slimy intestines. Trust me, a trip like that is sort of like going to Disney World—you remember it for a long, *long* time.

"I meant how you dealt with that SEAL, son. You met his anger with restraint."

"Thanks. I guess meeting Xanthos has mellowed me."

My father smiled. " 'Do not give sway to the negative way.' Good advice."

"Yeah."

"Giving you a little extra advice is why I'm here, son.

I'll be joining you from time to time on this mission, but strictly in an advisory capacity."

"Outstanding. I'll take all the advice you've got to give."

We moved closer to the mouth of the abandoned coal mine.

"I figured this would be as good a place as any to start searching for Mel and Abbadon," I said. "I think it leads to what Number 2 calls the underworld."

"It does," said my father. "But be on guard as you descend into Number 2's domain, son. You are about to enter a realm few have ever journeyed into. Fewer still have come back to talk about it."

My father vanished and I set up a homing beacon to guide in the fleet of helicopters.

As the landing skids slid across the windswept weeds of an open field and the heavily armed troops jostled out of the choppers, I materialized my four friends.

"So, Daniel, is this where you took out Attila?" Willy asked, surveying the scene.

"Yeah."

"Hey," said Joe. "The grease stain on that tree over there—is that him?"

I shrugged. "I guess."

"Gross, Daniel," said Emma.

Joe kept going. "And what about that oily splotch on that rock, and that chunky stuff dangling off that shrub, and that bony bit stuck in the mud?"

"Okay," said Dana, "that's just disgusting, Joe."

"I know! This guy Attila was all over the place. This

must be what they mean when they say you're spreading yourself too thin."

Agent Judge came jogging over to join us, followed by his 150-member strike force, all of them outfitted with serious alien weaponry clattering and clanking against their backs. My father wasn't there to greet his old friend, Agent Judge. In his role as special advisor to the team leader, he would be visible to and advising only me.

"So this is the place?" said Agent Judge, gazing down into the dark tunnel.

"Yes, sir. It was the initial rally point for Abbadon and his minions, right before they launched their attack on D.C. This mineshaft leads down to a cavernous chamber. That room could very well be an entrance to his underworld empire."

Agent Judge nodded and mumbled, "'Abandon all hope, ye who enter here.'"

He was quoting Dante Alighieri's *Divine Comedy*, an epic poem widely considered to be the preeminent work of Italian literature, about a previous descent into the devil's lair—what Dante called "The Inferno." That "abandon all hope" quote? According to Dante, it's the inscription right outside the front door to hell, which, if my hunch was right, was where we were currently standing.

"Lock and load," I shouted to the troops. They racked rounds into their weapons and charged up their whining blasters. I raised my hand and chopped it dead ahead at the entrance to the coal mine. It was time to begin our slow march into hell.

After about twenty yards, the sharply raked angle of the downward slope cut off all the daylight that had been streaming in through the squat entryway. We were plunged into total blackness. I blinked hard and switched my ocular nerves to their night-vision mode.

I could make out faint green blobs maybe another twenty yards in front of us. I closed my eyes so I could switch back to regular vision and shouted, "Light up your headlamps."

I didn't want my team stumbling around in the dark. I also didn't want to go blind when they all switched on the light gear strapped to their helmets.

When I opened my eyes again, I saw 150 shafts of tungsten light shooting through the misty gloom.

I also saw bats.

Thousands and thousands of bats. Startled from their roosts by the light beams, they flooded up the mineshaft.

"Take them out!" shouted Willy.

But before the strike force could squeeze off a single round, the bat swarm washed over us like a leaf-choked stream rushing down a sewer drain during a downpour.

"Hold your fire!" I shouted. We were completely swallowed up by a dense cloud of squealing, flying rodents. I could feel their fuzzy bodies and rubbery wings brushing across my face, arms, neck, legs—every inch of my body. Claws became tangled in my hair. This was no place for weapon fire. If we started blasting the bats, we'd be simultaneously blasting one another.

The swarm of flying rodents became so thick there was

barely room to breathe. We were more than surrounded. We were engulfed.

And then things got even nastier.

The thousands upon thousands of bats transformed into Abbadon's full-bodied alien henchbeasts.

And, believe it or not, they looked (and smelled) even nastier than they had as buck-toothed vampire bats.

Chapter 64

WE WERE OUTNUMBERED a thousand to one — no, more like *five thousand* to one.

"Hold your fire!" I shouted again.

Our targets were still too close. Yes, Agent Judge's handpicked team was full of brave warriors and skilled marksmen. However, very few of them had ever actually dealt with the kind of alien firepower they were currently carrying. A blaster gut-shot to the alien creep standing directly in front of you would bore straight through the creature's cockroach-crusty shell, shoot out his backside, and take out one of the mine's support beams, bringing down an avalanche that would bury us alive.

This is why blasters, when sold by legitimate dealers, come with warning labels: NOT RECOMMENDED FOR INDOOR USE.

All we could do was wait for Abbadon's slobbering lackeys to make the first move. And when they did, it wasn't the move I had been expecting.

They lined up in rows like a high school marching band, did an about-face, and started tromping down the subterranean passageway—*away* from us.

Were they retreating without firing a single shot? Then I noticed that none of the freakazoids were even carrying weapons. It was like they were a drill team without the toy wooden rifles.

And the weirdness kept getting weirder.

The massed legion of alien thugs, who moved like the synchronized marching machines North Korea likes to put on parade, pivoted their heads in unison and began chanting over their shoulders at us.

"Follow us. He waits below. Follow us. He waits below."

My new friend, Lieutenant Russell the SEAL, pushed his way to the front of our jumbled pack.

"It's a trap, Daniel," he said. "They want to lure you down there so they can ambush you."

"Maybe. But it's not an ambush if we're not surprised. I'm going down after them. The rest of you can stay here if you want, but I need to push on."

I started marching down the mineshaft, following Abbadon's followers.

Agent Judge, my friends, and the strike force?

They were maybe one or two steps behind me.

Chapter 65

WHEN WE REACHED the cavernous room where (ages ago, it now seemed) I had witnessed Abbadon's pep rally, I realized that this sweltering underground cathedral with its stalactite-studded ceiling was only the entryway into a vast and hidden labyrinth of passages.

My father, unseen by the other members of our force, including my four best friends, walked at my side as I followed the dark legions and descended farther and farther into the lower depths. Our conversation was telepathic. Nobody heard our thoughts except us.

Lots of legends about this place, he said. *Dante wrote of being lost in a dark wood, assailed by beasts he could not evade, unable to find the straight path out, falling into a deep place.*

I swiped away the sweat dribbling down my forehead. The deeper we journeyed toward the center of the Earth, the hotter it got.

You're feeling the effects of the "furnace of fire" the Bible speaks of, my father continued. *There is a reason hell is described as a burning wind, a fiery oven, and a lake of fire. The underworld is closer to Earth's mantle, a dense, hot layer of semisolid rock. It'll keep getting hotter the deeper we burrow.*

I had a feeling a lot of our strike force would be peeling off their tactical armor before we reached our final destination, wherever that might be.

Ancient civilizations knew of Abbadon's kingdom. For the Greeks, his home was known as Hades, an abyss used as a dungeon of torment and suffering.

When my father said that, I thought again of Mel.

Being held prisoner.

In Abbadon's dungeon.

And when I thought about her, I knew I had to keep pressing on, no matter how high the devil jacked up his thermostat.

When you encounter Abbadon—and you will, Daniel—trust none of what you hear, and less of what you see. Satan knows how to manipulate and deceive. There is only one way to defeat an adversary this cunning and shrewd....

Don't let him tempt me away from who I truly am, I mentally muttered.

Exactly.

Hours passed. We slogged on through the pressure cooker of heat and humidity, winding through a maze of narrow tunnels.

Our strike force was slowing down. The horde of aliens up ahead was not. According to Joe's radar sweeps, the distance between our two armies had grown to two, maybe three miles.

I'm growing weary, I heard my father say telepathically.

I never think of my dad as old, but right then he sounded ancient. Feeble.

Suddenly the cramped passageway we were shuffling through opened up, and we moved into an alpine valley beneath towering, snowcapped mountains—all of it eerily illuminated by glowing patches embedded in the earth, forty thousand feet above our heads.

"Incredible," said Dana. "It's like we're outdoors, underground."

"Only the sky is pitch black," said Willy. "And it looks like there's a couple hundred moons."

"Because that isn't the sky, and those aren't moons," said Emma. "Those are phosphorescent mineral deposits. We're looking *up*, at the Earth's crust."

"According to my readings, we're nine miles underground," Joe said, consulting his super-intelligent smartphone, which was loaded up with apps they don't sell in any store on Earth.

I used my 128:1 zoom vision to track Abbadon's blackhooded throngs.

"They're heading up into the mountains," I reported.

Then, son, said my father, *you better head up into the mountains, too.*

225

Chapter 66

JOE DID SOME reflected laser readings and simple triangulation geometry and confirmed what I already suspected: Number 2's minions were leading us up a mountain taller than Everest, the highest peak on the face of the Earth.

"The ascent, however," said Willy, "is more similar to K2, the *second*-highest summit."

That was not good news. K2 is a much more difficult and dangerous climb than Everest, with hanging glaciers clinging to the ridges near the summit and a narrow mountain gulley filled with ice and snow that rises at an eighty-degree angle. For every four people who reach K2's summit, one dies trying.

"We don't have time to acclimate to the altitude," Dana said, adding another problem to our growing pile.

I turned to Agent Judge. "It'd be suicide to march the entire strike force up the face of that mountain."

"What do you suggest?"

"That my friends and I go forward with two dozen of your top mountain climbers."

"We've got some airborne guys from the Tenth Mountain Division. And some of the Special Ops guys did time up in the Hindu Kush range of Afghanistan and Pakistan."

"Excellent. They're with us. You lead the others out of here. Backtrack the way we came in."

Agent Judge shook his head. "I'm not turning back, Daniel. Mel is my daughter."

"Yes, sir. But she's already lost her mother, and I refuse to allow this mountain to turn her into an orphan. With all due respect, sir, there is no way you can make the climb. And if you tried? We're all tied together on the safety line. You slip and fall to your death, you're taking people with you."

"I'm coming," said Lieutenant Russell. "We're trained to survive in extreme environments. Plus, I'm particularly good in low-oxygen situations. I can hold my breath underwater for three full minutes."

I grinned. I had to admire the guy's guts.

The thirty of us moving forward started our ascent up the craggy face of the mountain in the frigid air. Wispy clouds shrouded us in total darkness, taking visibility down to zero. Of course, I don't need to "see" to see, so I led the way. I had materialized crampons (spiked climbing shoes), carabiners, and climbing ropes—not to mention helmets, gloves, goggles, and tons of North Face thermal wear. We had left all the alien weapons with Agent Judge and the guys heading home.

So far, Abbadon's forces hadn't attacked us with overwhelming firepower. In fact, they hadn't attacked us at all. If things changed, I'd quickly create all the alien-frying heavy artillery we needed.

Snug in our webbed harnesses, tethered to a safety line, we were making slow but steady progress up the frozen face of the mountain. The strike force members were fit but fatiguing, fast. At high altitudes, starved for oxygen, muscles chill. Brains tend to turn to mush.

"Blue ice!" Willy shouted as he probed the ground with his ice ax, looking to secure another anchor. "We need to change course. Rappel under that overhanging glacier." He pointed to a three-hundred-foot-high hanging ice cliff, chunks of which could break off at any moment. "When we get to the other side, we scale the final four hundred feet up that steep ridge to reach the summit."

"Let's do it."

Dana and I were the first ones to swing from a dead snag over the jagged ravine that plummeted beneath the projecting prow of ice. With lines belayed, we brought the rest of the team across in their slings, one by one.

Until the giant block of ice broke and rained down frozen boulders.

The avalanche swept six of our brave warriors off the face of the mountain.

I stood staring down in horror at their crumpled bodies, scattered across the glacial plane more than fifty meters below.

"We press on," said Lieutenant Russell, who had been

the last man to safely cross before the rockslide, grimly. "It's what they would want us to do. It's for the salvation of our world." He gave one last look to the fallen, as if paying his last respects.

And then we did as he said and pressed on, shaken to the core by the horrible loss.

Hours later, twenty-four of us reached the summit, but there were no cheers of elation. A blinding blizzard immediately swept in and attacked us — a whiteout with winds that whipped our hard-shell climbing jackets like tent flaps in a tornado.

"Hang on!" I shouted.

The mountain rangers struggled to find hand- and footholds in the rocks.

"It's a fast-moving storm," Joe said, consulting the high-tech weather-radar app in his handheld unit. "It should blow through in a minute or two."

I just prayed it didn't blow away any more of our crew.

Ninety seconds later, just as Joe had predicted, the snow tapered off.

And moments after that, I felt water dribbling down both sides of my face.

Because all the ice that had accumulated on my goggles and climbing helmet was thawing, fast. So, too, was the snowcapped peak of the summit.

Like a freezer set to Defrost, the roof of the underworld was melting.

"What's the temperature, Joe?" I shouted across the roar of ice floes rapidly splitting apart.

"Ninety-eight. And rising!"

Chunks of ice and rock sloughed down the sides of the mountain, burying the passes we had taken on our climb to the summit.

We would not be going out the way we had come in.

Chapter 67

ON THE OTHER side of the mountain, an extremely flat and crackled plateau stretched out in front of us for miles. On the far horizon, I could make out a faint dotted line of black-shrouded henchbeasts marching toward the brightly burning sun.

"Um, what's the sun doing down here?" asked Dana.

"I think it's Abbadon's doing," I suggested.

"How?" said Dana.

"I don't know. Maybe the same way he magically dissipated my supposedly impenetrable protective dome."

"True," said Joe. "The smooth dude always seems to be one step ahead of you, Daniel."

"Two steps," Dana corrected. "Maybe three."

"Gee, thanks for the pep talk, you guys. Come on. We need to find his hidey-hole."

Willy, the best drill sergeant you could hope for, turned to the nineteen military men who were still with us. "Gentlemen, you were awesome climbing that mountain. How do you feel about crossing a desert wasteland?"

"An outstanding idea," Lieutenant Russell said, working his way out of his harness and climbing gear. "Desert conditions don't require nearly as much equipment."

"Hoo-ah!" shouted the rest of the squad as they started shedding their heavy climbing paraphernalia and winter parkas.

"We push on?" Willy asked.

"We push on," acknowledged Lieutenant Russell.

With Willy and me in the lead, my diminished squad began its long journey across the barren, parched plateau, which was crawling with giant scorpions, rattlesnakes, and poisonous spiders. The ground was riddled with cracks and fissures from baking beneath the withering heat of Abbadon's underground sun—which, by the way, never budged. Joe pegged the temperature at 110 and holding steady.

After hours of hiking, we noticed that the blazing ball was still holding its high-noon position in the sky. The strike force team members put on their military-issue wraparound shades and fashioned sweatbands out of fabric torn from their uniforms.

Fortunately, I was able to keep everyone's canteens filled with water just by imagining them full. But all the cool, refreshing water in the world couldn't stave off the exhaustion brought on by the unrelenting sun.

Eight hours into the desert trek, my lips were as dry and crackled as the ground we were crossing.

You are being tested, Daniel, I heard my father say as he slowly faded into view beside me. *This is all part of the game.*

You call this a game? *I lost six troops back there, and a half dozen more are ready to drop.*

That may be true, but this is still the game that's been played since the beginning of time.

I remembered the games my friends and I used to play. The fun we had jetting around on high-performance motorcycles. Playing with the elephants on Alpar Nok. Our round of extreme horseshoes, right before Abbadon's henchbeasts slipped through my defensive shield. What I wouldn't give to go back to Agent Judge's farm and play round two, only with Mel on my team this time.

My father, of course, could read *all* my thoughts, including the ones I'd rather keep to myself. He put his steady hand on my shoulder.

There is no turning back now, son. You must finally finish what we were sent here to do.

His words were strong.

His eyes were not.

My father was fading. And fast.

Chapter 68

THE MORE WE walked, the worse my father looked. I slowed down so he could keep pace with me.

"Everything okay, Daniel?" asked Dana.

"Yeah." I glanced over at her. The scar still marred her cheek. Now my father was barely able to keep up with me. What was going on with my powers to create?

Both Dana and my dad were products of my imagination. Was my father's deteriorating condition the result of my own deteriorating ability to generate his presence in the same way that Dana's scar hinted at some serious flaw in my imagineering operating system?

"We need to move a little faster, sir," Lieutenant Russell whispered to me.

Willy had finally spotted a patch of lush green foliage on the horizon. Some sort of oasis loomed one mile dead ahead.

"We need to get these men into the shade of those trees ASAP."

I nodded. "Roger that."

I turned to my father, whom only I could see.

Dad? We need to pick up the pace. Double-time it to those trees.

My father looked drawn and haggard. His eyelids kept drooping shut, like he was sleepwalking. I swear he had aged fifty years in the last fifty minutes.

Well, if you're in such a dag-blasted hurry, go on without me, he snapped. *I'll catch up later.*

He sounded crankier than the crabby old man on Alpar Nok who used to sit on a park bench and yell at me for squealing too loud in my zero-gravity crib. This wasn't the real Dad I'd known, and it wasn't the imaginary Dad I usually created. Something was seriously wrong.

"Willy?" I said.

"Yeah?"

"Lead everybody into that grove. I'll catch up with you in a few."

"Everything okay?"

"Yeah. Get moving."

"Ladies and gentlemen," Willy called out, "if we push ourselves for one more mile, I guarantee we can peel off our boots in a beautiful oasis and tickle our toes in a cool, refreshing stream!"

"Hoo-ah!" the troops shouted as strongly as they could after climbing a mountain and crossing a desert. Chanting a running cadence, they trotted off after Willy, Joe, Dana, and Emma.

My father and I were all alone at the rear of the march.

235

"When we get to the oasis," I said, "I'll rest. Recharge my batteries. If I feel better, you'll feel better."

"It's not an oasis," my father grumbled. "It's a jungle."

"Well, it looks cooler than this desert plane."

"It's full of insects, Daniel. Bugs. I hate bugs."

Of course he did.

When Number 1 killed my father and mother, he came at them in the guise of a giant praying mantis.

Was it any wonder my father had a thing about insects?

Chapter 69

WHEN WE FINALLY reached the jungle (yes, my father had been correct), the strike force had already pitched tents under the dense canopy of trees and set up camp for the night.

I was about to drop my backpack to the ground and machete my way through a tangle of vines to do the same when my father shook his head.

"We need to talk," he said.

"About what?"

"Everything." He looked around, most likely surveying the average number of bugs per square inch in our current surroundings. "But not here. Follow me. And bring your backpack."

I followed my father through the dense underbrush. He led me to a sun-dappled clearing situated between four mammoth banyan trees with thick, woody trunks strangled by snaking air roots. My father sat cross-legged in front of me and gestured for me to sit down.

"You see the four trees to the north, south, east, and west?" he asked.

"Yes, sir."

"They say Buddha achieved enlightenment while meditating under a banyan tree. So, too, shall you."

"What do you mean?"

"As much as I'd like to stay with you, son, I can't journey at your side forever. In the hours we have left, I need to tell you everything you must know."

"Okay..." This was weird; it meant that Dad knew a lot he'd never told me before. Why would he keep secrets from his only son?

"Let's start with the deity we know as Number 1," he began. "For eons, this twisted god has been amused by the eternal struggle between good and evil, the never-ending battle of demons and angels, darkness and light."

"Destroyers versus creators," I added.

"Exactly. Number 1 has always favored the dark side, but more than anything, he enjoys watching a good fight between equally matched opponents. So, to keep things interesting, he pits the universe's finest creators against its deadliest destroyers. It's also why Number 1 gave us The List."

My jaw dropped. "Whoa. Wait a second. You expect me to believe that my ultimate nemesis, The Prayer, the creep who holds the number one ranking on The List of Extraterrestrial Outlaws on Terra Firma, is also the guy who *gave* us that list?"

"Yes, Daniel. Believe it." The silence of my overwhelming disbelief was pretty deafening. "In fact," my father continued as I tried to absorb all of this, "Number 1 not only gave us The List but is also the one who constantly updates it."

I was glad I was sitting on the ground. Otherwise, I might've keeled over. This was absolutely incredible. For his twisted entertainment, Number 1 made sure that we Alien Hunters/Protectors from Alpar Nok always knew where to find the most hideous creatures from all over the galaxy, who had come to Terra Firma to spread death and destruction.

"Did he enjoy watching me take down Attila outside the bat cave?" I asked.

"I'm sure he did."

"And what about Number 19, back in Portland? The one that was part man, part jellyfish, and part chain saw?"

"I'm sure Number 1 was greatly amused."

"So, what? He's like Zeus up on Mount Olympus, looking down from his lofty throne and drooling with delight as mere mortals fight to the death for his enjoyment?"

My father nodded. I thought about all the alien baddies I had hunted down and bumped off The List. Especially Number 6, the planet annihilator who, years earlier, had killed the real Dana, Willy, Joe, and Emma back on Alpar Nok.

Now I was learning that my mission had been Number 1's *entertainment*. My battles, struggles, and sorrows were all just exciting new episodes of this deranged deity's favorite action-packed TV show.

"When I refused to fight Number 2 in Kansas," my dad continued, "Number 1 demanded that I give him back The List."

"Why didn't you just call off the game and give it to him?"

"Because I knew you would need The List to protect this planet, Daniel. The other side, the alien outlaws, had no intention of calling it quits. As we grow older, Daniel, we realize that, when things don't go our way, we can't just pack up our toys, call it quits, and head for home. If I had surrendered The List, Earth would have been destroyed several times over."

"I know. But if Number 1 really wants a fair fight between me and Number 2, why does The List draw a total and complete blank on Abbadon?"

"Does it?"

"Yeah. There's nothing about his planet of origin, his—"

"Look again, Daniel."

"What?"

"No more secrets. The time has come. You need to know *everything*."

Chapter 70

I REACHED INTO my backpack and pulled out the sleek, paper-thin laptop I hadn't consulted since my last visit to the bat cave, when it kept coming up blank on Number 2.

I swiped a fingertip across the glass screen and the ultra-secret Wiki about superpowered psychopathic aliens whirred to life.

"Number 2," said my father.

The computer obeyed his command and started rapidly shuffling through its mug shots of alien outlaws like the flying-album-cover view on iTunes. Two seconds later, the montage stuttered to a stop on a hideous image of Number 2 in his full demon mode.

Beneath the picture, I now saw *tons* of information.

Number 2. AKA ABBADON, SATAN, THE PRINCE OF DARKNESS, THE DESTROYER, IBLIS, BEELZEBUB, ANGRA MAINYU...

The Known Aliases list scrolled on for several pages.

Apparently, The List had gone from knowing nothing all the way to TMI.

KNOWN PHYSICAL APPEARANCES.

I just skimmed this section, since I had already seen Number 2 shape-shift his way from winged-back demon to a smooth newscaster to the grim reaper. The guy was the great pretender, the great deceiver, *and* a quick-change artist.

Finally, the screen filled with the information I had been desperate to discover.

When I read it, I sort of wished it was still a blank.

PLANET OF ORIGIN: Alpar Nok.

I looked to my father. "He's one of us?"

"Yes, Daniel. He commands the same incredible powers that you do."

"He can use his imagination..."

"...to destroy whatever you can create with yours. He can make you see things that aren't really there. Think things that aren't really true."

I nodded slowly as I mentally cataloged my own incredible superpowers. Not the standard comic book action-hero stuff, like my super speed, X-ray vision, and level-three strength. I didn't even focus on my ability to rearrange matter and create whatever I could imagine.

No, I was thinking about what my dad had just mentioned: *how I can mess with minds.* I can make people see things that aren't really there, and think things that aren't really true.

So, apparently, could Number 2.

Was my Alpar Nokian cousin playing mind games with me?

Did the Washington Monument really come tumbling down, or was that image just in my head because Abbadon planted it there?

I closed the laptop. There was no need to check out the list of Evil Deeds Done, as my father had already shown me the horrible things the one called the devil had done throughout human history.

My father stood up. "Daniel, you now know all that you will need to know to complete our family's mission on this planet."

My head was still spinning. "Number 2 is really one of us?"

"He comes from the same planet, Daniel. But that does not mean he is the same as you and me."

"But Dad, how do we take down an Alpar Nokian who can match us move for move?"

"That question has not yet been answered. You, Daniel, are the one to answer it. It is your destiny."

"But you'll help me, right?"

"No."

"*What?*"

"You don't need my help any longer, Daniel. It's why my physical presence seemed to fade today. Why you saw me aging into a tired old man."

A single golden shaft of sunshine somehow beamed its way down through the thick canopy of jungle foliage over our heads and lit up our banyan-tree clearing.

"Yeah, I didn't want to say anything. I thought maybe you forgot to take your vitamins or something."

My father smiled. "My mission as your father is complete. My spirit must move on."

"But you'll come back, right? Because even if I don't need you anymore on this mission, we still need to hunt down Number 1 and—"

"No, Daniel. This is our final conversation. I will not be returning to this realm, in body or spirit, *ever again*."

Impossible, I thought.

No way could my father be totally abandoning me.

Yes, physically, he died all those years ago back in Kansas. But spiritually, his presence has manifested itself whenever I've needed it to.

"That's just it, Daniel," he said, having read every one of my jumbled, panicked thoughts. "You don't *need* me anymore. You're ready to live life on your own. You don't have to imagine me back into existence. Use that energy for something more important."

"But—"

My father held up a hand to gently silence me. "Before I depart, I want you to know something, son: I'm extremely proud of you."

I felt a huge lump in my throat.

"After what happened in Kansas, no one would've blamed you if you went into hiding for the rest of your life. Instead, you found The List and set out to fulfill your own Alien Hunter destiny. Along the way, you've done for complete strangers what no one could *ever* do for you. I'm so sorry you had to grow up all on your own, Daniel. I truly am. But you know what?"

I managed to get out a faint "What, Dad?"

"You did an amazing job."

All I could do was choke back my tears as my father's body seemed to start glowing, like a radiant sheet of gauze.

And then he said his last words: "It has been my honor and privilege, my greatest accomplishment, to have been part of your life."

That was it. My father became a shaft of golden light and disappeared into the dusty sunbeam illuminating our secluded grove.

In my heart, I knew the truth: he would never be coming back.

Chapter 71

ALL THAT WAS left of my father was a faint sprinkling of silvery dust.

I stood there staring down at it, trying to make him come back, focusing all my creative energy on one task that used to be so simple—bringing him back.

Because I forgot to tell my father how much *I* loved *him*.

"He knows," my mother said as she drifted into the lush tropical garden. "Those ashes are the physical remains of his essence, Daniel. His soul has already moved on to its next great adventure."

"This isn't fair. He can't die on me *again*. I can't lose my father twice!"

"That's one way to look at it, I suppose," said my mother. "Or, Daniel, you could marvel at how fortunate you were, for so many years, to have the power to be with him even after he died. Think of how many people, young and old alike, would do anything to have a second chance with their departed fathers and mothers."

I nodded. She was right.

"Let's gather up his ashes," said my mother. I heard a slight catch in her voice.

"Are you okay, Mom?" I asked. It was kind of a dumb question, under the circumstances.

In fact, she was starting to look older, too. Her golden hair seemed thinner. Less shiny. Grayer.

"Help me, Daniel."

I steadied her by the elbow as she knelt on the ground and lovingly scooped up the feathery ashes, placing them in the crook of a fallen banyan-tree leaf. I knelt beside her and helped.

"I'm so sorry, Mom."

"Thank you, Daniel. By the way, have I ever told you how much I love you?"

"Only every day. And I love you, too, Mom."

"I know, dear. Your father knew it, too."

She folded up the leaf holding my father's scant ashes.

I stood and once again steadied her as she creaked up from the ground.

"I sensed death was coming," she said with a sigh. "I just didn't know for whom."

"I was hoping it would be Abbadon."

"One day it will be his turn. None of us are gods, Daniel. We are not immortal."

"What about Number 1, The Prayer?"

"Yes, you're correct. That creature *is* different."

"He's probably watching us right now."

"Then let's show him how much we loved your father.

247

Let's cast his ashes to the winds. We all came from stardust, and to stardust we must return."

My mother opened the folded leaf and blew a breath
across the grayish powder that had once been my father.
The wind carried it away and, when it hit that single shaft
of sunshine, I swear the tiny particles sparkled like a galaxy of stars.

"And now, Daniel, I must ask you to do the same
for me."

My heart sank to my sneakers. "What do you mean?"

"Your father and I were soul mates, eternally linked
across all time and all dimensions. When one soul leaves a
realm, its soul mate will never be too far behind."

Now she became translucent, just like my father had;
her body was a glowing paper lantern of golden light.

"Wait," I said. "Don't leave me all alone."

"You're never alone, Daniel. We'll always be with you."

She disintegrated into a sparkling cloud and drifted off
on the wind. When her dust hit the sunbeam, the sandy
particles glittered for an instant, then disappeared.

My mother wouldn't need me to collect her ashes.
She was already on the wind and, like my father, wouldn't
be coming back.

Suddenly I felt the same way I'd felt when I was three
years old. Racked with shuddering sobs, I felt the same
gut-wrenching agony I had felt when The Prayer stole into
our Kansas home and took away every good and happy
thing I had ever known.

I had just been orphaned for the second time and,

believe me, it hurt just as much as the first time. Maybe more. Because I had been given the chance to know my parents as people.

I heard a rustle in the underbrush. I looked to my right and saw Lieutenant Russell.

He came closer and stood beside me. He didn't say a word. He didn't have to.

We were two warriors who dealt with death on a daily basis. And yet we both knew that some deaths hurt more than others.

Because the souls closest to our own take some of us with them when they leave.

Chapter 72

UNDER ORDINARY CIRCUMSTANCES, I would have given myself a little more time to mourn my father and mother.

But I was operating in the anything-but-ordinary zone known as the underworld, a parallel landscape lying miles beneath the surface of the Earth. After what felt like days spent climbing ice-capped mountains and crossing a barren desert, I was certain we weren't under West Virginia any longer. Joe's best guess, after he consulted his geotracker app, was that we were somewhere under Mexico. Or the middle of the Atlantic Ocean. Or maybe Canada.

Apparently, the churning movement of the Earth's liquid core was playing havoc with the magnetic field and throwing off the accuracy of all his compass readings.

Now, two hours after my parents made their final exits, my friends, my remaining troops, and I had trekked through the sweltering jungle and stood at what looked like the vine-covered entrance to a Mayan temple. One slab of the igneous rock basalt—lava that had been heaved up and rapidly cooled—stood supported, Stonehenge style, by two other basalt columns, forming a doorway into the darkness. The gray, oblong blocks had strange hieroglyphics chiseled into them, symbols that even I, with my encyclopedic knowledge of runes and symbology, couldn't translate.

"This cave definitely needs a crate of Tic Tacs," Joe said as a stench that went beyond putrid surged out of the cavern's mouth.

"Or we could hose it down with a tanker truck full of Listerine," suggested Dana.

The suffocating stink was, we suspected, strong enough to kill. Two soldiers who had volunteered to scout the entryway passed out, succumbing to the noxious fumes.

"Gas masks!" shouted Willy. Those of us still standing slapped on our protective gear.

When we raced forward to retrieve our comrades, jets of gaseous dragon fire shot out of the tunnel as if it were a gigantic blowtorch.

"Erm, Daniel," said Joe, when the firestorm finally subsided, "maybe now would be a good time to turn back?"

"What?"

"Well, my friend, I think we've discovered the actual gates of hell."

"Not a place that's ever been on my must-see list of earthly attractions," added Dana.

"Abbadon is down there," I said.

"Daniel and I are going in," announced Willy. "Who's coming with us?"

"I guess this is why they say the road to hell is paved with good intentions," Joe quipped as he stepped up to join us.

Emma and Dana were right behind Joe, with Dana remarking, "It's like they say: If you're going through hell, keep going."

Lieutenant Russell and the remaining members of the strike force fell in behind my friends.

We were all moving forward. Together, to the end.

As we entered the eerie gloom of the sweltering shaft, each member of my squadron knew the harsh truth hanging over our heads: another fire blast could shoot up the tunnel at any moment and incinerate us alive.

Because this wasn't just a parallel world.

This was a parallel nightmare.

Chapter 73

AS WE JOURNEYED deeper into the unknown, we started encountering trapped souls of the damned.

The first group—whom we encountered in a chamber where Joe pegged the temperature at 120 degrees Fahrenheit—were people who, basically, did *nothing* in life. They weren't good, but they weren't really evil, either. They didn't even bemoan their eternal fate in this sweat-box. They were blasé blobs.

I remembered what Dante had written: "The hottest places in hell are reserved for those who, in times of great moral crisis, maintain their neutrality."

"Let's keep moving," I called out to my squad, all of whom were gawking at the silent specters surrounding us. The souls of the "uncommitted" swatted at wasps and hornets swarming around their heads. They tried to swipe away the maggots and leeches ferociously sucking on their flesh.

We left them to their eternal misery.

James Patterson

After passing through this vestibule, we boarded a ferry-boat and crossed a black underground river.

"Next stop, hell," droned the ferry pilot. "Hell is next."

I looked at Lieutenant Russell. He actually grinned. We were both remembering the vow he'd made after our martial arts match: *Heck, kid—I'd follow you into hell itself.*

We now entered a series of terraced, circular rooms spiraling down in receding levels. It was kind of like the Guggenheim Museum in New York City—only the walls were black and slick and slimy.

The first circle was crowded with souls who simply looked lost or confused.

"I did nothing wrong!" cried a woman. "Why am I stuck in limbo?"

The second circle down was full of those who had been overcome by lust. I recognized a few dead politicians and celebrities, all famous for cheating on their spouses.

We continued down the wraparounds, as if we were trying to get out of a parking garage.

The next circular chamber was filled with souls wallowing in filth, like pigs, while raw sewage dribbled on their heads.

"Why are you here?" I called out.

"In life I was a glutton. I ate like a pig. All day, every day!"

I realized that Dante had been spot-on in his description of the circles of hell. So, having uploaded his masterwork into my memory banks at the age of six, I knew that beneath the gluttons would come the avaricious and the prodigal; that is, people who had spent their lives chasing

254

money. In hell, they had to chase after one another with giant boulders.

The level below that, the fifth circle, was a swampy place—an open cesspool where those whose lives had been filled with rage had to wrestle one another in a pool of chunky brown muck. If you ever visit the fifth circle of hell, trust me—you want to pack nose plugs.

We looped down to the sixth circle, which was filled with heretics (those who disagreed with official Church teachings), and wound our way into the several sub-rings of the seventh circle, where all sorts of violent souls were spending eternity splashing around in a river of boiling blood. In every circle, consequences were paid in death for choices made in life.

"Um, Daniel," whispered Dana, "can we pick up the pace?"

"Please," Emma agreed. "This is like a freaky seven-ring circus."

"It's amazing," I remarked as we entered a vast, open space I knew had to be Dante's Abyss. "He got it all right."

"Who?" asked Joe.

"Dante."

"Why are you so amazed, Daniel?" purred a smooth voice from the darkness. It wasn't any of my friends. Unfortunately, I recognized it all too well.

Abbadon!

"Of course he got it right. Signor Dante came to visit, and he took excellent notes."

Finally, Abbadon (or Number 2, Satan, Lucifer, or

Beelzebub—the guy had more names than a champion show dog) stepped into the dim light of the cavernous room. All I could see of his face were two red eyes glowing in the black circle beneath the hood of his robe. Apparently, Abbadon was going with his grim reaper look again.

"And now, finally," he said with a sigh, "*you* are here. Welcome, Daniel. Welcome!"

I could hear his raspy, rumbling breath quicken in anticipation.

"By the way, I heard about your mommy and daddy. What a pity they both had to die—again. On the same day. *Again.*"

In the blackness beneath his hood, I could now see his slick teeth glisten as his lizard lips slid up into a smile.

And then he laughed.

It was the most hideous laughter I have ever heard.

Chapter 74

WE WERE ONCE again engulfed by a swarm of Abbadon's loyal followers.

My friend Lieutenant Russell pulled out his wicked-looking survival knife. One edge of the blade was razor sharp; the other was serrated for sawing into meat. He meant to take down as many henchbeasts as he could before they opened fire and splattered his guts against the cave walls.

"Stand down," I ordered.

"We can take these guys, Daniel," Willy encouraged me. "There's only, what? A couple thousand of 'em?"

Okay, you have to admire Willy's fighting spirit, if not his odds-making abilities. But we were totally outnumbered, and I couldn't bear to see any more brave souls die on this journey.

We had found Abbadon. As far as I was concerned, the quest was over. It was time for Number 2 and me to give Number 1 the fight he had been craving for centuries:

Daniel vs. Abbadon. Two evenly matched Alpar Nokians in a one-on-one, no-holds-barred, knock-down-drag-out fight.

"This is between him and me," I said.

"I agree," Abbadon declared, raising his cloaked arm and flicking his wrist.

My four friends and the remnants of Agent Judge's strike force vanished.

"Where are they?" I demanded.

"Let's see . . . the four imaginary figments of your childhood friends have once again drifted off to their own special limbo. The others? Well, Daniel, I sent *them* back to the surface of this dying planet so they can experience, firsthand, the final moments of its miserable existence."

Chapter 75

I WAS SURROUNDED by Abbadon's drooling thugs, but with another flick of his wrist, all of his minions disappeared, too.

It was just him and me, staring at each other across the cavernous void.

I had no friends, no family, no strike force. I had never been so completely, utterly alone.

Number 2's red-hot eyeballs throbbed with excitement. I heard a wet smack as his tongue slid across his lips.

The devil was *so* ready to give me my due.

To make matters even worse, I couldn't imagine any possible escape. I had no idea how to defeat this beast who could match me move for move, weapon for weapon, transformation for transformation, while seeming to have absolutely no weaknesses of his own.

Suddenly, a last-ditch idea came to me.

Like all those about to enter the arena to face their fiercest rivals, I needed to study my opponent's game films.

I flashed back to what my father had said when he'd filled the walls of the barn with flickering images of Number 2's evil exploits:

Study him, Daniel. Study everything he does — and I mean everything. Every movement, every gesture, every telling smile. Look for his weaknesses.

It was time, once again, to follow my father's advice.

So, first I said a quick prayer that Number 1 hadn't (as he had in the past) put up a disruption field around the planet to prevent time travel.

And then I dove under the rippling surface of the temporal plane and zoomed back to 1942, when Abbadon rode with the Nazis in Amsterdam.

Chapter 76

I WAS HOPING to meet Miep Gies.

Hey, I knew that studying Abbadon's past actions (killing, looting, plundering, and causing global devastation) was going to be pretty tough. At least I could try to restore my faith in humanity by seeking out one of history's heroines while I was at it.

Miep Gies was one of the Dutch citizens who hid Anne Frank, her family, and several other Jews from the Nazis during World War II. She was also the woman who found and preserved Anne Frank's diary after the Franks were arrested in their hiding place—a secret attic above Mr. Frank's spice factory in Amsterdam.

Gies and her helpers could have been executed if they had been caught hiding Jews. But they did what they knew was right. You don't find those kinds of souls wandering around in Abbadon's circles of doom.

I was walking up Amsterdam's Prinsengracht, the longest of the city's main canals, toward number 263—the building where Mr. Frank had his spice mills and warehouse. I glanced at a newspaper drifting across the cobblestones. It was August 4, 1944.

Not the date I would have picked.

"Why not?" crooned a voice behind me.

I whipped around.

It was Abbadon. He was right on my tail!

"Did you really think you would find my weaknesses in the past, Daniel? Such a foolish boy. The past contains some of my greatest victories! This day in particular has always been one of my favorites," he sneered. "This is the day in the Frank family saga that clearly proves my point: evil always triumphs. If it didn't, hell wouldn't need so much real estate."

I heard a commotion up the street. Nazi soldiers and gestapo men in black trench coats were storming into canal house 263.

August 4, 1944, was the day Anne Frank and her family—after hiding from the Nazi occupiers for two years—were finally captured. Anne and her sister were taken to the concentration camp at Bergen-Belsen, where they both died a few weeks before the British Army liberated the camp.

Three weeks earlier, she had written what would become the most quoted entry in her famous diary: "It's really a wonder that I haven't dropped all my ideals, because they seem so absurd and impossible to carry out. Yet I keep them, because in spite of everything I still believe that people are really good at heart."

My feelings exactly.

But it was hard to picture people being "good at heart" with the Lord of the Flies himself, Abbadon, standing there, grinning triumphantly at me. He was dressed up in an appropriate period costume: a black fedora and a black leather trench coat with a swastika wrapped around its left sleeve. The red of the armband matched his sinister eyes. He laughed mercilessly when the German secret police roughly removed the Frank family from 263 Prinsengracht.

"Poor little Annie," he said with a sigh. "It seems a petty thief who has fallen on hard times called the authorities this morning. Ratted her out. Can you blame the poor soul? He desperately needed the reward money."

"There is good in this world!" I shouted.

"Oh, I suppose you will find a bit of it scattered here and there, Daniel. But when all is said and done, these accursed creatures would gladly watch you die if it meant *they* might live another day. Why do you think so much of humanity has already fled to my side while you were left to fight for the planet's future with, what? Four make-believe friends and a pathetic, hodgepodge assortment of overzealous soldiers?"

"This wasn't the day I came here to see!"

"No," sneered Abbadon. "But it was the one you *needed* to see."

"You sent me here?"

"For your own good, Daniel. After all, we're cousins."

Things just kept getting worse.

How could Abbadon's creative powers override my own? How could he continue to force me to see things I had no desire to see?

I had time-traveled into the past hoping to find his weaknesses.

Instead, I found another one of his strengths: He could redirect my own creative abilities. He could mess with my mind!

I definitely needed more information on this creepy cousin before I went up against him in a death match. I could think of only one place left to find it: our common home.

Alpar Nok.

So while Number 2 stood there disgustingly admiring the Nazis, who would someday be joining Abbadon in the circles of hell, I streaked off into outer space.

Chapter 77

MY FIRST STOP back home was an unbelievable zoo I know inside a hidden park beneath the universe's biggest shatterproof solarium.

I went to a vantage point overlooking a grasslands field filled with herd upon herd of elephants. The friend I was seeking saw me first. She approached my viewing platform very gracefully—especially for an elephant that weighs forty, maybe fifty thousand pounds. She extended her telephone pole–sized trunk to me and I gently stroked it.

Welcome back, Daniel, she said in my mind.

This was Chordata. I had known her as an infant and met up with her again when I set out on my first alien-hunting adventure.

Why do you look so anxious, my young friend?

I need your help.

Then my help you shall have.

Remember how you told me an elephant never forgets?

Well, if I couldn't remember saying it, how could it possibly be true?

I grinned. *Have you ever heard of another two-legged Alpar Nokian who calls himself Abbadon? He's been on Earth for centuries, maybe since the dawn of human history.*

Ah, yes. The Fallen Soul.

You knew him?

No. He is far older than I. But I have heard the stories. It is a cautionary tale we still tell our children. A story of one who was given tremendous talents and powers, who, instead of using those gifts for a greater good, chose instead to selfishly enrich and prolong his own life. You see, Daniel, the one known as the Fallen Soul was granted not immortality but a vastly extended life by an evil god known as The Prayer. So long as the Fallen Soul did that god's bidding and provided him with constant amusements, he would be granted life.

I had wondered how Abbadon could've hung around Earth for so many years if he was truly an Alpar Nokian, like me. Yes, we live a very long time. But thousands of years?

Well, I communicated to Chordata, he's been keeping up his end of the deal, putting on quite a horror show for The Prayer's amusement. But now he's upping his game. He aims to wipe out the entire planet. And he's doing a pretty good job of it. Now he's eager to destroy me, too.

You say he destroyed the planet?

Yes. The civilized parts. I saw buildings topple. Whole cities were leveled. The Four Horsemen of the Apocalypse rode across the rubble.

Are you sure of this, Daniel?

I saw it with my own eyes.

Ah. Then perhaps it did not happen.

I shook my head to clear out the bafflement. *Huh?*

Always remember, Daniel — the fallen one has the same powers you do. He can conjure up a reality and make you see it through the sheer force of his destructive imagination — especially if certain fears already lurk in your subconscious.

My father had said something very similar about Abbadon: *Trust none of what you hear, and less of what you see.*

So the cities of Earth aren't really leveled?

They might be, Daniel — so long as the one you call Abbadon imagines that they have been.

I was beginning to understand.

The things I create with my imagination only stay that way as long as I focus my creative energies on them. If I release an object or person from the grip of my transformative powers, they go back to being what they always were. I could not alter their essence, only their substance. Trust me, it'll make sense one day, after you've read Aristotle's *Metaphysics* or spent a little time in Plato's Cave.

I leaned down and gave Chordata a quick kiss on her wet snout.

What was that for, Daniel?

Hope. You've given me hope!

Talking to Chordata, I finally realized that if I could defeat Number 2, then all the destruction he had conjured up with his twisted imagination would be erased the instant I erased him!

There was only one problem: How could I do that?

How could I defeat him?

There was only one place I hadn't looked for the answer: the future.

Yes, it was a pretty sketchy, highly questionable idea, but I figured it might be my last chance to find some flaw in my nemesis. Maybe I could go just far enough into the future to watch our fight and see how he'd come at me, and then flip back to the present knowing how to foil his attack. Maybe I could see him kill me and then zip backward in time to stop it from actually happening on the do-over.

Yes, it was complicated, but then again, saving a whole planet from imminent annihilation usually is.

I concentrated every fiber of my being, every molecule in my body, every ounce of my creative powers on recalling exactly how it felt when Abbadon had sucker-punched me into the future. It was time to re-create that moment.

Using cellular-level sensory recall, I blasted forward. . . .

Into the future.

Chapter 78

I WAS NEW at fast-forwarding, and unable to completely control exactly when (or even where) I reemerged in the time line.

So I didn't end up in the abyss, Number 2's chosen arena for our final confrontation.

Instead, I was once again in Kentucky. In the barnyard.

"Daniel? Are you going to wear *that* for our ride?"

Mel, looking maybe three or four years older than I remembered her (okay, looking like the cutest high school girl you can imagine), came out of the farmhouse in her riding clothes. "Seriously," she joked. "You look like an Abercrombie & Fitch catalog... from five years ago."

So far, except for my geeky clothes, I liked what I saw in the future.

For one thing, Mel was there.

"Have you saddled up Xanthos?" she asked.

Don't forget my blanket, my brudda, said a familiar voice in my head.

Awesome thing two about the future: my trusty white steed and spiritual advisor, Xanthos, was alive again. What Chordata theorized was true: once I destroyed Abbadon in our death match, I also erased all his destructive imaginings.

"Hey, kids," shouted Agent Judge from the back porch. "I packed you a picnic lunch." He was holding a little wicker basket.

Awesome future thing three: Agent Judge, and hopefully most of his strike force, had survived their trek out of the underworld.

"I put in a couple of cartons of that new Coke you both love."

Awesome future thing four? A new kind of extremely refreshing organic Coca-Cola in eco-friendly, biodegradable packaging.

"We'll come back for it, Daddy," said Mel. "We don't want the food to get all wet when Daniel falls in the creek again."

"Hey," I protested playfully, not completely recognizing my own voice. It was deeper. Richer.

Awesome thing five: I'd conveniently skipped all that awkward puberty junk. Guess I was all grown up, too. Probably a high school senior, like Mel appeared to be. I definitely wanted to find a mirror so I could make sure my last few pimples had faded away like everybody promised me they would.

Okay, there wasn't much in this future to help me fight Abbadon back in the past except, of course, the knowledge that good (me) had somehow triumphed over evil (him). Plus, I saw flowers blooming. Heard birds chirping. Smelled the sweet smell of newly mown grass in the air.

And, standing over by a greeting card–caliber wishing well, I saw both my mother and father.

They were holding hands and waving at me. I swear there was a rainbow in the sky behind them.

"Did you really think we could stay away forever?" joked my father. "Oh, and by the way, Daniel, I'm reading an incredibly interesting book about antigravity. It's impossible to put down."

Yep, it was definitely him. The corny pun sealed the deal.

I dashed across the barnyard.

"How about we have pancakes for supper tonight, Daniel?" said my mother, sounding perky and chipper, the way I remembered her. "Your sister will join us."

"Is Pork Chop here?" I asked eagerly, even though she could be the most annoying little sister in the galaxy.

"Not yet," said my dad. "She had some sort of after-school water-ballet recital with the sea lions back home on Alpar Nok. But she'll be coming down for dinner."

"I'll tell Agent Judge to set another place."

As I said that, I glanced down into the well, hoping to check out my reflection in the smooth, glassy water.

But when I looked down, I didn't see myself.

I saw him.

Abbadon.

He had followed me into the future, too!

Chapter 79

"YOU SILLY, SENTIMENTAL sap." Abbadon's rippling image sneered up at me from the dark well water.

Suddenly I didn't smell springtime anymore.

I smelled foul sulfur and raw sewage and rancid, maggot-riddled hamburger meat.

I yanked my head back.

Abbadon was standing on the other side of the wishing well, which had transformed itself into an express chute down to the underworld. A jet of gaseous flame rocketed up from the silo, charring the rune-inscribed stones circling the mouth of the well.

I looked back to the barn. It was on fire, roiling with flames and billowing black smoke. Beneath the roar of the blaze and the crackle of popping timbers I could hear Xanthos's strangled screams.

Mel was gone. So, too, were Agent Judge and my parents. In their place, I saw a zombie army of wretched souls dripping sludge carried from the muck pits in the fifth circle of hell, stumbling around the barren wasteland that had, seconds earlier, been lush meadows. Locusts and giant termites with wingspans the size of condors' swarmed around the farmhouse and devoured it.

"I wanted you to see the future of your dreams, Daniel. That way it would hurt all the more when you realized you will never, ever live to see such things. The future, dear cousin, belongs to me!"

The four horses of the Apocalypse came charging out of the burning barn, their manes dripping fire. Abbadon pulled another four-way split and mounted his abominable steeds. The four hideous horses, each one spurred on by a different Abbadon, circled me in a dizzying blur of black, red, white, and pale green. I was trapped—penned in by a swirling wall of colored horseflesh, stomping hooves, and Number 2's maniacal laughter.

Then, just as suddenly as it had started, it stopped.

Abbadon and I had made a joint leap in time and space to the windswept planes of the abyss beneath the dome of the underworld.

"Of course, Daniel," my enemy cooed seductively, "your future doesn't have to end up quite so bleak. I am more than happy to share this planet with you. Just renounce your silly solemn vow to wipe out the alien outlaws inhabiting Terra Firma."

I shook my head. "No thanks."

"Why are you so stubborn, Daniel? Surely you have seen that these pathetic humans crave the darkness more than anything else. They long to be rich and comfortable and stuffed with food—to be just a little better off than their weakling neighbors. I can give them this, Daniel. And I can give it to you. Serve me and become one of Earth's most pampered elites!"

An army of docile servants joined us in the abyss. Maids, waiters, and butlers. Coachmen, masseuses, and limo drivers.

Beneath the servant uniforms, I recognized many of the human faces I had seen in Washington and elsewhere, the ones who had been the first to stampede down into the safety of eternal slavery.

"Can I polish your shoes for you, Mr. Daniel?" groveled one of the eternally enslaved.

"No thanks. They're Nikes."

"Some pancakes, perhaps?" cried out a fawning woman in a maid's uniform. She held forth a platter piled high with a stack of hubcap-sized flapjacks that were dripping with butter and syrup. "I used your mother's recipe."

"Sorry, but I'm pretty sure you left out her secret ingredient."

"Tell me what it is, and I'll add it!"

"Nope. Like I said, it's a secret."

Abbadon snapped his fingers. The submissive ones disappeared.

But a new man joined us.

I recognized him immediately: the leader of the *gopnik* in Moscow.

The young Russian street tough who had scarred Dana's face with the broken vodka bottle!

Chapter 80

"YOU REMEMBER YURI," Number 2 cooed.

"Yeah," I said. "We've met."

"Would you like to kill him, Daniel?"

I felt something materialize in my hand.

It was Lieutenant Russell's survival knife.

"An eye for an eye, a tooth for a tooth, a cheek for a cheek," said Abbadon.

"Actually," I said, tossing the knife to the ground, "I believe they revised that one. If someone strikes me in the cheek, I'm supposed to offer him the other one, too."

A second knife materialized in my hand.

It looked even more deadly.

"Forget all your antiquated morals, Daniel. In my new world, killing is not a sin. In fact, we encourage it. If someone strikes you, you are perfectly free to murder him."

I tossed the second knife away, too. If I became who

Abbadon wanted me to be, sure, I'd be alive, but would I want to live with myself?

"This is your lucky day, Yuri," I said to the Russian, who was leering at me with hate in his eyes. "I'm not going to kill you, no matter how much your new Lord and Master begs me to."

Number 2 tsked. "Are you really that cowardly, Daniel? You won't fight to defend your lady's honor? Not much of a man, are you, boy?"

"You are a wimp," the Russian said with a grin. "The wussy."

Abbadon's face filled with glee. "Did you hear what he called you, Daniel?"

I could feel my ears burning. Rage surged through my veins. Abbadon, who moved like a magician, waved his hand.

The Russian raised his jagged bottle and said, "I am going to cut your other girlfriend next."

"Oh, ho, ho!" said Abbadon. "Should I let him have a few moments alone with Miss Judge, Daniel? Shall I take this Russian lad to Melody's cell?"

"You leave her out of this," I snarled.

"That's it, Daniel. Feel the hate. Feed on it. Take your revenge for Dana. Protect Mel! Strike this useless bag of Russian bones dead. Do it now!"

I bent down and picked up the knife. The grip felt good in my hand.

"Before I mark the girl," the Russian boasted, "she and I

will have some fun." He puckered up his lips and blew fish kisses at me.

Okay. I seriously wanted to do in the Russian sleazeball.

More than anything in the world, I wanted him to pay the ultimate price.

Chapter 81

REMEMBER HOW I said Abbadon moved like a magician?

Well, this wasn't some kid's birthday party, and I wasn't going to become his willing volunteer from the audience.

That rage rushing through my limbs and up into my head? I knew who put it there: Abbadon. It's an Alpar Nokian mind trick, where you make somebody think *they're* feeling emotions when actually *you're* the one making them feel that way. How do I know this? I've used it myself in the past. It's highly effective. Unless, of course, your target knows they're being targeted.

So I focused on the knife I held in my hand and transformed it into a Frisbee, which I flung at the Russian. He caught it with his left hand and, furious, came at me with the jagged bottle in his right.

When his fist came up toward my face, I grabbed his arm and locked it in place.

So it would be easier for me to sniff the lovely bouquet of flowers he was offering me.

Yeah, that's right—I rearranged the bottle's molecules.

"Flowers?" I said. "For me? Why, Yuri, I didn't know you cared."

The Russian thug didn't look so tough clutching an FTD Sweet Splendor Bouquet.

"You dare mock me?" thundered Abbadon.

He swept his arms up over his head, and the imaginary Russian hoodlum crumbled into a heap of gravel.

"Trust me, Daniel, you will beg to join me before I'm through with you."

"Doubtful," I said. "But go ahead. This is your rodeo—show me what else you've got."

That's when the magician played the most hurtful card in his hand: Mel!

Chapter 82

SHE WAS IMPRISONED inside a tiger cage of translucent force-field bars.

"Are you okay?" I shouted.

"I'm fine!" It was amazing to hear her voice. It had felt like centuries, somehow, since we'd talked for real.

I rushed toward the cage—

And was immediately blown back by a jolt of a couple thousand gigawatts.

It knocked me down, but I bounced right back up. Inching forward, I heard the surging throb of the high-voltage electrical charge. Mel was only ten feet away, but with the impenetrable force field between us, it might as well have been ten miles.

"I'm sorry, Daniel," said Abbadon. "Until you fall to your knees and worship me, I can't allow you to come any closer."

"Don't you dare do as he says," Mel said, feisty as ever. "Don't even listen to him!"

I gazed into her sky-blue eyes. For that instant, Abbadon wasn't even in the room. It was just me and Mel.

"Has he hurt you?" I asked.

"No. But he lies like the devil."

That made me grin. "Yeah. There's a reason for that...."

"You know, Daniel," snapped Abbadon, "you and Melody could be quite happy together."

"We know that," I said. "But having you around kind of ruins all the fun."

"Not necessarily. If both of you swear your allegiance to me, then I give you my word: the two of you can go back to Kentucky and live like normal, ordinary teenagers. No more of this 'protector of the planet' nonsense. Why, you could prance about on ponies all day, every day. And then, when evening falls, you could hold hands and take long, moonlit strolls down to the malt shop."

I arched both eyebrows.

So did Mel.

The malt shop? Abbadon was showing his age. I don't think anybody's gone on a date to a malt shop since Archie and Jughead were chasing Betty and Veronica.

But Abbadon was playing this temptation through.

As Mel and I stood frozen in disbelief, we saw duplicates of ourselves riding white horses across a creek. The other Daniel and Mel were laughing, having a grand time.

I even fell out of my saddle, right on cue, and went splashing into the creek.

"Ride much?" said the duplicate Mel with a gentle laugh.

"Um, not really," said alternate me.

"You know, Daniel, you're even cuter when you're soaking wet," said duplicate Mel, giggling, as I started peeling off my T-shirt and flexing my chest muscles like a junior Schwarzenegger. Abbadon definitely needed to hire some new scriptwriters for his alternate-reality soap opera.

I'd seen enough. "You mean we could become puppets for your amusement. Strike two, Abbadon. No sale."

"Fine," said Number 2. "Have it your way!"

And then he attacked me with everything in his arsenal.

Chapter 83

I GUESS YOU could say I had won the first two rounds.

Well, at least I *survived*. Abbadon couldn't break me, mentally or emotionally.

So, for round three, he was just trying to break me.

As in, *every bone in my body*.

He hurled me off a cliff and down the jagged side of a mountain. My body was racked with pain as my limbs shattered, my spine crunched, my joints popped, and my head throbbed. All I could hear were my own groans and my internal organs smashing into one another.

Abbadon had transformed me into a rolling boulder.

"Surrender to me, Daniel!"

"*Never,*" I grunted, as best I could.

When my body—now made of rock, but somehow filled with all the sensation of a fragile human body—hit the boulder-strewn ravine five hundred feet beneath the jutting cliff, I bounced once, then burst into flames and became a rolling fireball. The pain was indescribable as every bit of my body burned, an inescapable inferno. The punishment went beyond gruesome. This was sheer torture.

"And it will go on for all eternity, Daniel," gloated Number 2. "After all, this *is* hell! And you haven't even begun to know pain yet."

When my rocky meteorite of a body finally came to a stop, Abbadon snapped his fingers and turned me back into myself. But the flaming boulder didn't disappear. I lurched forward, no longer in control of my body, and started to push the boulder back up the mountain.

I almost preferred plummeting down the cliff to this unparalleled agony. Abbadon may have been forcing me to push, but he wasn't helping me with the massive weight at all. My broken bones intensified the horror, the impossibility of it all.

Somehow—stumbling, falling, almost crushed by my task—I reached the top of the cliff, after a stretch of time that could've been minutes, hours, or years.

And then it got even worse.

Abbadon turned me back into the boulder and hurled me off the other side of the mountain, my punishment becoming a never-ending cycle of pain.

Up.

Down.

Up.

Why hadn't Dante written about *this* circle of hell in his *Inferno*?

On my third crash down the cliff, I saw that Abbadon

had found yet another way to blast pain through my whole being.

It was Mel.

Like me, she was being forced to roll a boulder of jet-black onyx up the mountain. When she got to the top, her body transformed into rock, like mine had, and started rolling down the other side of the cliff.

I was so messed up at that point I thought I even saw her flattened face pressing against the glassy-smooth surface of the stone as she flew by me in a lightning flash.

One thing I *know* I didn't imagine, though: I could clearly hear her anguished cries for help!

Chapter 84

HEARING MEL'S WOEFUL cries ripped me up. Badly.

My spirit was nearly shattered, my will almost broken.

But, somehow, hearing Mel also reminded me of who I truly am.

The creator. The Protector.

The Alien Hunter who can do whatever I can imagine.

Mel had given me the strength to become myself again.

So when I rolled my boulder to the summit for the umpteenth time, I caught a glimpse of Abbadon, standing on a precipice with his arms akimbo, laughing triumphantly.

Hey, whatever he could do, I could do. Right?

So I imagined *him* becoming a boulder and cascading down the cliff right behind me.

But it didn't happen.

On my return trip up to the summit, I imagined Number 2 blown to smithereens.

I mentally depicted every detail of his bodily explosion.

Still, it didn't happen.

"Give it up, you weakling!" Number 2 shouted as I plummeted off the cliff again. "I can sense your feeble creations the instant you attempt to generate them. You are a disgrace to those of us who truly know how to use the gifts we have been given."

I bounded back up.

Abbadon kept smirking at me.

"You know, Daniel, it's a good thing your mother and father have already departed this realm. They would be absolutely appalled to see how unimaginative you actually are."

I tumbled down the mountainside as Mel groaned and gasped on her way up.

I could hear what was left of our unbroken bones crunching. I could hear her whimpers as the boulder's flames licked her skin.

Abbadon kept mocking me: "This is why your mommy and daddy left you all on your own, Daniel."

I hit rock bottom and immediately started my return up the harsh slope.

"They could no longer endure the prolonged embarrassment of having *you* as their only son. Ha! They're better off dead!"

I neared the top of the cliff.

Number 2's taunts should've stung worse than bashing my bones against the boulders below.

But they didn't.

Because he had just told me how to beat him.

Chapter 85

THE ANSWER WAS right there in Number 2's barbs and jeers.

My mother and father.

Yes, they were brave and fearless, incredibly talented, loving, and strong.

But in the end, they died anyway. *Because they were not immortal.*

My mother had practically spelled it out to me over our last breakfast together: *Death is always with us, Daniel. None of us is immortal. Eventually, we must all depart this realm and move on to the next.*

Chordata, up on Alpar Nok, had given me the answer, too: *The one known as the Fallen Soul was granted not immortality but a vastly extended life by an evil god known as The Prayer.*

Even Xanthos had been dropping hints back at the stables: *We are all mortal. Otherwise, we would be gods, no?*

As a last gasp—and I mean that literally, because I didn't

288

know how much longer I could keep drawing breath after all that unfathomable pain—I *imagined* Number 2 dead.

I saw his soul being reduced to stardust and blown away on the wind.

I saw it and felt it and grokked it with every cell, every molecule of my being.

I had never focused so intently or so fiercely on any of the transformations I had pulled off in all my years as the Alien Hunter. I was giving this single vision every ounce of energy I had left.

If the metamorphosis didn't kill Abbadon, it would surely kill me.

But why wasn't he fighting me back? He said he could feel my meager imaginings and stop them easily. Was it because he couldn't imagine himself dying? Did he think it was so impossible that even I couldn't imagine it?

Big mistake.

I reached the top of the cliff just in time to see Abbadon roar as he burst into oily flames.

"NOOOOOOOOOOOOOOO!" he screamed. "NOOOO NOOO *NOOOO!*" And suddenly he was in my head, fighting back with everything he had. But it was too late. My imagination had captured him, and his long life of destruction was finally over.

Instead of sparkling gold particles, his soul exploded into gleaming black specks of soot. At first he looked like a swarm of angry black flies clustered in the shape of a body. But then a stiff wind blew across the abyss and shot his inky essence skyward.

Fanned by the oxygen-rich gust, the cinders of Abbadon's soul began to glow and then burn, turning as fiery red as his eyes.

In an instant, what was left of Number 2 became the flaming tail of a comet streaking up through the dome of the abyss, which, when Number 2's mind faded into oblivion, became what it really was: the black, starlit sky.

The same thing happened to me and Mel.

Released from the grip of Number 2's evil imaginings, we were two teenagers again, standing in a grassy meadow, watching a shooting star racing away from Earth.

Abbadon lit up the night sky like a sizzling fuse stretched across the heavens until the instant the thin line of his essence burned out and the sky went black.

"You finally found his weakness," Mel said as we held hands and stared up at the twinkling stars.

"Yes," I said.

"What was it?"

"He wasn't a god. He was like us. He was mortal."

Chapter 86

I SUDDENLY REALIZED where we were: Kentucky. At the Judges' horse farm.

"So, Daniel, has anyone ever told you that you're amazing?" said Mel. Then she rocked up on her toes and kissed me on the cheek. "A very impressive first date."

"Um, this was a date?"

"Well, we got to see that cheesy movie about our happy future. So, is your chest really that buff, or were those special effects?"

I was about to answer when I heard a voice in my head. *Welcome back, brudda.*

"Xanthos!" I cried out loud.

"What?" Mel said as we both started running toward the barn. "He's back from the dead?"

"I don't think he ever died."

"Yes, he did. They made me watch them kill him when they kidnapped me."

"I don't think that ever happened, either."

"Uh, yes it did. I was there."

"I know, but, well...I think Abbadon put all this in our heads, the way I do sometimes."

We tore into the barn, and there he was—shaking out his snowy mane, pawing at the hay, giving us a happy whinny.

So, Daniel, you did not give sway to the negative way. Yah, mon?

I laughed and said, "Yah, mon," right back at him.

I noticed a paint-spackled portable radio perched on a shelf outside Xanthos's stall and switched it on, hoping to get confirmation that my theory was correct.

A newsreader came on: "And down in Washington they're getting set for a spectacular fireworks extravaganza. With all of D.C.'s monuments and the U.S. Capitol in the background..."

I turned the radio off.

"Washington wasn't destroyed?" Mel said, sounding confused.

"Well, it was—as long as Number 2 imagined it was."

"And now that he's gone..."

"Washington isn't."

"So you just basically saved Washington, New York, London, Beijing, Moscow...okay, the whole planet?"

"Yeah."

"Incredible!" And she hopped up to give me another kiss.

Now Agent Judge strode into the barn, followed by Lieutenant Russell. They cleared their throats to announce their arrival.

"Um, hi, Daddy," Mel said, blushing a little.

"You're both safe?"

"Yes, sir," I said. "And as far as I can tell, everything on Earth has gone back to normal."

"I'll say," said Lieutenant Russell, shooting me a wink.

"Daniel?" said Agent Judge.

"Yes, sir?"

"I'm mighty impressed, son. Your parents would be proud."

"Thank you, sir."

When he said that, I remembered that my father and mother were gone. Forever.

Abbadon didn't imagine them away. They had left on their own.

Life was really going to be different from here on out.

Chapter 87

ABOUT AN HOUR later I sat down in the meadow and stared up at the blanket of stars.

Number 2 was gone, erased from this realm for all time.

But if a fellow traveler from Alpar Nok could truly become the devil, what was I meant to become?

I had so wanted to slay that Russian gangster for what he had done to Dana. Did the rage and hatred that fueled Abbadon burn inside me, too?

I needed to talk to my parents.

Maybe they didn't mean it when they said they were going away, never to come back.

"Dad?" I whispered. "Mom? I still need you."

I closed my eyes and focused on their presence.

When I opened my eyes, I was still alone. In a field. Under the stars.

So, it was true. I couldn't summon my parents.

Fine. I'd hash this all out with my friends. I summoned Willy and Dana, Joe and Emma.

They didn't come.

"Look, you guys, I don't even care if Dana and Willy are dating now or whatever. I need to talk."

Still, they didn't come.

A lump formed in my throat as I realized I was completely and utterly alone on Earth. A stranger stranded in a strange land. Being the Alien Hunter had taken a heavy toll on me. I had given up everything I ever had. My family. My friends. My shot at a normal life.

For a moment I wondered if I had also given up my incredible superpowers by forcing Number 2 to surrender his. Were we so linked, like the two sides of a coin, that what happened to him happened to me?

No, mon, said a friendly voice in my head. *Otherwise, you would be stardust instead of staring at the stars, yah?*

Okay, I wasn't completely alone. I still had Xanthos, my spiritual advisor.

"Are you okay, Daniel?"

And, yes, I had Mel.

She sat down next to me.

"I was kind of worried when you disappeared from the dining room."

"Guess I'm just not in the mood for ice cream tonight."

"How about we go out for a malted?" Mel cracked, remembering Abbadon's corny idea for a hot date.

"I'll take a rain check," I said with a smile.

"Thought you might want this." She held up the slim computer that had been my main alien-hunting tool. "You left it inside."

"Thanks," I said, "but I don't really need to look at it. Number 1 is next. Number 1 has always been next."

I hoped Number 1, The Prayer, had enjoyed watching Number 2 and me battle each other in our Armageddon death match. I figured Number 1 should stay tuned, because his own personal Armageddon was coming up...right after the break, as they say on *American Idol*.

For some odd and insane reason, that made me smile.

So in my next battle, I'd be going up against some kind of alien god, right?

Fine. I'd brush up on my Greek and Norse mythology. Read a few more Percy Jackson books.

Feeling better than I had in a long time, I draped my arm around Mel's shoulder.

We gazed into each other's eyes.

And I noticed something I had never seen before.

"Did Abbadon do that to you?"

"This?" She pointed at a long scar on her cheek. "No, Daniel—it's always been there."

And that's when I finally realized what I should've known all along: the reason Mel reminded me so much of Dana was because she *was* Dana.

It's pretty amazing where souls can journey when they leave one realm and enter the next.

And how true soul mates can never stay separated for long.